PASSAGEWAYS

THE LIVING WORLD
BOOK ONE

PASSAGEWAYS

THE LIVING WORLD
BOOK ONE

Patricia Vestal

Sea of Mountains Press
North Carolina, US

Passageways: The Living World Book One by Patricia Vestal

Paperback ISBN: 978-1-7375849-1-9

Published by Sea of Mountains Press, North Carolina, USA
www.seaofmountainspress.com

For permissions contact:
Website: seaofmountainspress.com
Email: author@seaofmountainspress.com

Cover and book design by: Michelle Triggs Owen, www.ProjectDesignInc.com

Cover image credit: NASA, ESA, N. Smith (University of California, Berkeley), and The Hubble Heritage Team (STScI/AURA)

DEDICATION

Dedicated to those who cherish all living things.

PASSAGEWAYS

THE LIVING WORLD
BOOK ONE

CHAPTER ONE

Jeff Hawke had just taken a giant bite from his tuna melt when he heard a warm female voice floating over the clamor of the busy coffee shop.

"Mind if I sit here?"

He gazed up through the dark locks tumbling over his eyes at the most perfect creature he had ever seen. Standing behind the chair opposite him, she gave him a dazzling smile. He pushed back the wayward hair from his face and swallowed the chunk of food in his mouth. Was it possible for anyone to look like that?

She continued with a hint of humor. "This place is packed. Do you mind? I won't bother you."

Jeff dropped the sandwich back onto the plate without taking his eyes off her. "Oh, uh, sure. Help yourself. Yeah, it always gets like this here at lunch." He hoped that tuna wasn't smeared on his face.

She slid into the chair. "Thanks. Can you recommend some-thing, uh, vegetarian?"

"They have a tasty hummus on pita with sprouts." Jeff waved at the waitress, watching her grab a menu and weave her way toward them between crowded tables.

"I can order now," the woman across the table said, gracing the waitress with her smile. "I'll have the hummus on pita and water. Thanks." She turned to Jeff, "Don't mind me, just go ahead with your meal. You're probably on a schedule."

Jeff forgot about the food. He just wanted to stare at the vision before him. It was like she stepped out of his dreams: tall and graceful; long, bouncy auburn hair; an oval face dominated by luminous green eyes. He was wracking his brain for something to say, maybe find a way to see her again. "Yeah, I work at police headquarters. Always too crazy over there for much of a lunch break." There, that seemed natural enough. "You work around here?"

"I'm a journalist on assignment here." She seemed amused by the way he arched his eyebrows.

"Oh yeah? That's interesting. What kind of assignment?"

She smiled. "You're a policeman. I don't know if you'd find it interesting."

"I'm not a regular cop. I'm more of a techno-geek." Jeff's inner voice groaned. *That was a stupid thing to say. What's wrong with me?*

Her eyes widened. "Oh, that's fascinating. Somewhat related to my topic. Maybe you can help me."

A leap of confidence buoyed Jeff. "I'll try."

"I'm looking into artificial intelligence, the state of the art in the field, and, well, whether we're being a little blasé about any potential danger. I mean, there are obviously benefits, but also, you know, pitfalls, risk, that sort of thing."

"Whoa, that's pretty heavy. Well, we do have several types of robots at headquarters. They're sort of rudimentary. Can't see them ganging up on us." He chuckled. Dumb joke. "I don't mean to ridicule your work. I do think you'll need to talk to some pretty rarefied scientists. You must already have people lined up, though." His voice trailed off. I sound like a dope. The arrival of her sandwich gave him a chance to reboot the conversation. "I lean toward vegetarianism too." Dumb. Now I sound patronizing.

"I'm glad to hear that." She took a small bite from her sandwich. "I'm Tami Graves."

"Jeff Hawke. Nice to meet you, Tami."

"I haven't lined up any interviews yet, although I've done quite a bit of research."

"You might want to try the universities. They're top rate." He slapped his forehead. "Hey, that's probably why you're here." Jeff felt like he'd been spewing out verbal gaffes. He tried another topic. "Are you staying nearby?"

She hesitated. "I have a hotel room. I hope to find time to look for a bed and breakfast, someplace homier. I might be here a while."

Jeff beamed. "I know just the place."

"Really? Where?"

"It's centrally located. Name's Dream Catcher."

"What a beautiful name. Isn't it Native American?"

Jeff squirmed. "Well, actually, yes, it is. A cousin of mine owns it. She is, well, Cherokee, like me." He bit his lip, wondering what made him say that.

She seemed intrigued. "It sounds like the perfect place for me. How do I get there? Or should I call first to make sure there's a room?"

Jeff took out his cell. "I'll call my cousin now." He was rewarded with another amazing smile.

■　　■　　■

The Dream Catcher was just right. Convenient, but secluded and set back in a stand of ancient trees. Her room faced a backyard pond. Tranquil. A suitable place to take a break from impersonating a human.

Now in her natural energy form, she shifted her amorphous essence across the room, thankful for the respite.

"Ms. Graves." A voice and knock at her door roused Tami. "I'm serving wine and cheese in the great room, if you'd like to join us." It was Sarah Hawke, the proprietor.

She hastily formulated her human voice. "I'd love that. I'll be there in a few minutes."

■　　■　　■

Fellow Synons called TuMa'Aye Gra'Vay, aka Tami Graves, Queen of the Realm.

In her natural energy form, she had traversed one of the Passageways by which the Realm was tethered to Earth. Synons employed ambient energy and matter to formulate objects and mold themselves into material semblances of animals or people, which they called personas.

The Realm had no physical attributes. It was a universe held together by the collective beings that inhabited it—Synons, comprised of energy, mind, and spirit. Their purpose was to maintain and strengthen the link between The Living World that encompassed all of Creation and Earth's life, especially the dominant species, humans. That human bond to The Living World needed constant reinforcement; it was fraying at an accelerated rate that threatened the very existence of Earth's life and the Realm. The Realm itself was fraying. Tami's mission was to discover how and why that was happening.

■　　■　　■

"Jeff says you're researching artificial intelligence." Sarah handed Tami a glass of Merlot, taking the chair across from her.

"Yes, I'm a journalist." Tami sipped the wine. Synons could simulate eating and drinking. They repurposed the matter into energy in a much quicker and more efficient manner than biological digestion and metabolism.

An older couple sat on a love seat, both cramming cheese and crackers into their mouths. The man managed to swallow and wipe his mouth before speaking. "What publication are you working for?"

Tami tensed. There was something distasteful and suspicious about these two. She was unable to penetrate their minds, which was not unusual with self-absorbed humans. Here, she hit what seemed like a deliberate block. She needed to deflect this line of inquiry. "Uh, they've asked me to keep that confidential. In fact, I've probably already said too much about my assignment."

The man snorted. "Too late for that. How much science fiction is out there about runaway robots and killer machines?"

"My assignment is to take a strictly analytical, scientific approach. I'd like to get better acquainted with you. Is this your first visit to the Dream Catcher?" Tami found it hard to focus on the conversation. She suddenly was exhausted. Her mind felt sluggish. She obviously had not yet perfected processing wine into energy.

"Yes, it is." The woman spoke in a rather timid voice.

"Would you like some more wine, Mrs. Jordan?" Sarah brandished the decanter.

"Oh yes, I would. This is delicious." The woman, suddenly not so timid, eagerly held out her glass. Her husband's hand reached out and pushed the glass away. "Thanks, Miss Hawke, but we have a dinner engagement. Miriam, we should be going." He addressed his wife with a hint of harshness as he rose and offered his hand to help her up.

Appearing flustered, Miriam set her glass on the table and took her husband's hand, finding her manners and her voice. "Thank you, Miss Hawke. This has been lovely."

After they had gone Sarah mused, "A typical couple of their generation. He leads. She follows. Reminds me of why I'm still single." With a wry smile and toss of her voluminous head of hair, she sipped her wine.

"I'm also single." Tami's mind felt more alert. She sensed an opening to learn more about Sarah, who looked at least a decade older than Jeff and seemed comfortable in her bohemian style. "How did you come to own this lovely inn?"

"I inherited it from an uncle. At first, I was just going to sell it. I'm not a city person. Then, when I came down here and visited the place it just seemed to grab me and say, 'Stay.' I've never regretted giving up a less than glowing career as a dental assistant."

"That's a nice story. Where did you come down from?"

"Cherokee. That's why I studied dental hygiene. I wanted to do something to be of use to my people."

"You grew up in the Native American culture?" Tami wanted to know more about this part of Sarah's life. The Native Americans' link to The Living World was ancient and genuine, like that of all indigenous and nonurban people whose lives were innately tied to natural surroundings.

"I did. Yet my life wasn't that different from most girls living in small towns. The difference for me was that my town happened to be a tourist destination because of its wonderful mountain location, and people are interested in our story. They have, of course, been fed much laughable and harmful—what we today call misinformation—about Native Americans. Tourism has provided enough prosperity that we've been able to develop authentic and entertaining ways to tell others about ourselves." She chuckled. "Of course, tourism also attracts commercial trappings. Other tribes have similar and dissimilar stories."

"Of course." Tami nodded, hoping to display understanding. "There isn't one Native American culture. Although there are similarities, each tribe has its unique story."

"I'm so glad you recognize that." Sarah smiled. "The Eastern Band of the Cherokee purchased our land in the 1800's, and it's kept in trust by the federal government. It's called the Qualla Boundary. Cherokee is a city within the Boundary. We have our own democratic government but are U.S. citizens as well."

"Your people were badly treated yet you don't seem bitter."

"I recognize that history is filled with stories of prejudice and ignorance, greed and cruelty. I can never speak for anyone else. I try to make each day the best I can for anyone I can."

"A fine philosophy. And you're achieving that by providing this haven for travelers."

Tami lifted her wine glass. "Cheers." She paused momentarily. "You grew up in Cherokee, then came down here to take over this inn you inherited from your uncle?"

"He was a restless young man, wanting to make his fortune. And then he finally wound up here as innkeeper just like he easily could have if he'd stayed in Cherokee." She laughed. "And here I am. Maybe we can't really escape our fate."

"Indeed," Tami mused.

CHAPTER TWO

Once again ensconced privately in her room, Tami thought, not a bad start, replaying the events that had brought her to this moment.

With her power dwindling, TuMa'Aye Gra'Vay shrank herself as small as she could, taking the form of a cockroach, crouched next to a puny tree amid a sea of concrete. The ground trembled as monstrous moving machines rumbled nearby.

The urge to search for another Synon was irresistible. She tried to focus, straining to touch Synon essence. Silence. Was she alone? She grasped only miniscule amounts of energy emanating from the natural environment. This harsh, inhospitable environment humans had created on Earth had abruptly closed the Passageway behind her, sealing her off from the Realm and depleting her power. Over the eons Synons had learned how to use their powerful mental capabilities to simulate a biological body and to access sources of sensory input. Now a draft of pungent air tugged at the roach who was TuMa'Aye Gra'Vay, and she toppled forward, almost catapulting into moist, pulsating nostrils.

TuMa'Aye Gra'Vay recognized a variation of one of the many languages she had absorbed through prior visits to this planet. An irritated female voice rang out, "Max, come on, you can't poop there."

The nostrils retreated. "Hello?" The dog, curious and confused, sensed TuMa'Aye Gra'Vay's presence. Then he was gone, trotting alongside his person. The brief encounter between them had, however, given TuMa'Aye some of her strength back. She transformed to a fly and summoned the verve to explore her surroundings.

TuMa'Aye Gra'Vay saw that humanity had scarred the Earth when she crossed into one of its most obnoxious examples: a modern city. She couldn't know that this one was among the least offensive. On her most recent visit to this place, only a few hundred years before in Earth time, she had encountered a pastoral setting populated by small bands of people, whose connection to The Living World kept the membrane between the Realm and Earth unobstructed and strong. Were these people gone? Or had they simply changed? The chasm between then and now was peculiar; it helped explain why the connection was gradually closing, leaving only a few Passageways. Combined with Synons who had come to Earth on various missions, then ceased to communicate with the Realm, and were possibly closing Passageways, the situation was dire. At this point TuMa'Aye Gra'Vay recognized what appeared to be a twofold challenge. Her mind saw patterns. Suppose resident Synons had become influenced by humans and were disregarding their mission? She forged on with renewed purpose.

Navigating through chaotic streets filled with noisy crowds and fumes from moving machines that were new to her, she followed a faint trace of the natural world to an expanse of grass and trees linking walkways that seemed to be made of hard material similar to that which covered the streets. Despite the artificial-looking low grass and the symmetrical arrangement of trees, the place emanated a surge of positive energy. The air was charged with laughter and excitement, with people strolling along the paths, running or riding two-wheeled contraptions; children were playing on various structures built to their scale. Humans still needed a tether to the natural world, miniscule as it was within the larger metropolis. Perhaps here she could find an ally.

TuMa'Aye Gra'Vay absorbed much-needed energy from the natural life around her, taking in the splendid sunset and the enveloping cosmos, its stars obscured by the city glow. As the green place emptied and the babble of people enjoying the evening died out, she allowed herself to change from a fly to a tiny mouse ready to nestle under a bush. Something heavy and warm slammed down on her, and a sharp-clawed paw poised to slap her. A tiny squeak escaped her. "Stop!"

The claw retracted. "What are you?" It wasn't words, only emanations of a primal psychic link. She looked into curious, huge green eyes as a feline rested his chin on the ground before her. A cat.

"I speak for The Living World. I need help."

The cat's head cocked slightly. "Hop on."

TuMa'Aye Gra'Vay hopped onto the outstretched paw and scurried up the leg onto the velvety black shoulder, burying herself in the warm security of the cat's neck fur. She had found an ally.

Riding the cat let TuMa'Aye tap into his memories, showing her how he had been abused and abandoned by people. It was an example of the myriad ways by which humans hurt each other and the beings with which they shared the Earth. This constant onslaught posed a great danger to The Living World.

"What is this place called?" she asked the cat.

"It's a park."

Fueled by the surge of energy from the close contact with ambient life, TuMa'Aye was able to take on the form of a beautiful tiger-striped cat. She found herself facing a group of motley feral felines. "Is there anything about this place I should know about?"

An orange tabby with mottled ears gazed at her. "People in uniforms come here at night in noisy moving things to take away others sleeping in the park."

"So there are still people who command others?" TuMa'Aye asked, reflecting on her prior visits.

"That's right," one of the other cats offered. "And they don't like homeless cats either."

"Follow this path toward the bright lights," the orange tabby said. "You'll find better sources of energy there."

She thanked them and pranced away on four white paws. A sliver of moon was the only heavenly body not obscured by the glow of city lights. TuMa'Aye opened her awareness, becoming one with the vegetation around her. When she followed a path that turned into denser vegetation, a different, distressing awareness intruded. Bodies huddled on benches. Murmurs and even a cackle of laughter drifted toward her, and a child whimpered.

As if on cue, chaos erupted. "It's the cops! Run!" Benches sprang to life and blankets were flung on the ground. Shouts. Scuffles. Curses. Cries. The child screamed. People scrambled in all directions, only to be rounded up by those who had arrived in machines flashing colored lights and were rending the quiet with shrieks.

TuMa'Aye Gra'Vay transformed into a fly, buzzing past the melee to her destination, a shiny black and silver moving machine. She watched a burly woman drag over a young girl, who in turn gripped the screaming child—a shocking and dismaying sight. When the female enforcer opened the door, shoving in the girl and the child, TuMa'Aye flew inside and huddled on the floor.

A new experience ensued as doors slammed and the monster roared and rumbled beneath her, then lurched into motion. Thanks to the strong grip Nature bestowed on flies, TuMa'Aye managed to hang on until the machine stopped and its doors opened in front of a large building. She flew out and followed the people dubbed "cops" who were herding the homeless from the park into the building.

■   ■   ■

Buzzing within the chaos, she gleaned fragments of information from erratic tiny bursts of psychic connection.

Then an explosion—a direct link into a kindred mind poured information about this place into her awareness. The young man strode through the crowd greeting cops with smiles and hand slaps. When TuMa'Aye's mind touched his, he halted and looked around curiously, then resumed his trek, not noticing the fly following him. The brief touch of his mind gave TuMa'Aye enough information to know that he had entered the technical control room, an environment new to her yet comprehended through knowledge that instantly flowed from his mind to hers.

As he closed the door behind him, the ambience changed into quiet dimness, with soft whirring mechanical sounds and rows of glowing screens that her dip into the young man's mind told TuMa'Aye were computers; men and women were sitting in front of them. The young man approached a woman at a workstation and tapped her lightly on the shoulder.

She swiveled in her chair and greeted him with a warm smile. "Hi, Jeff."

"Thanks for pinch-hitting, Marie," he said, brushing the dark locks of hair from his eyes.

TuMa'Aye watched with curiosity as Marie rose toward Jeff but didn't touch him, even though an invisible force seemed to be pulling them together. TuMa'Aye knew instinctively that these two shared a bond that neither of them fully understood or acknowledged.

"No problem," Marie said. "Hope your training session went well."

Jeff seemed to mirror her behavior, radiating warmth but keeping her at arms' length. "Sure did. Maybe I helped a few cops learn to use their electronic toys without getting hacked." He laughed and glanced at a clock on the wall. "Hey, looks like my shift's nearly over."

Marie gave him an update, sealing it with another smile. "See you tomorrow." And on that, she grabbed her bag and left the room.

TuMa'Aye lit on the back of the chair Marie had just vacated, quickly zooming off when Jeff sat down and leaned back, almost squashing her with his shoulders. She hit the first available surface, the glowing screen.

Jeff swatted at her gently trying to shoo her away. "Hey, how'd you get in here?" He conveyed none of the malice humans usually directed toward flies. As TuMa'Aye swooped away the next man to spot her exuded a more murderous intent. TuMa'Aye darted through a nearby door into what her yield from Jeff's mind told her was the server room. Monolithic racks of computers surrounded her like a glowing primeval forest. Reams of cable were like multicolored vines growing everywhere. She squeezed through a tiny ventilation opening in the center unit, keenly aware of the current of power so near, flowing like a river. She followed one of these tributaries to its port of entry into the landscape of silicon and metal. In her pure energy form she should be able to swim this current into the mysterious ocean of knowledge that she sensed within. Its siren song called to her. TuMa'Aye surrendered to the overwhelming urge to do the unthinkable and abandon her material form, letting her pure energy meld with the data stream that coursed within the machinery. It deluged her with its essence.

Was this a new entity? It was unlike any that had ever existed on Earth. She sensed an almost omnipotent presence, but no life force or spirit. And yet, this thing that she perceived was called the Internet encompassed intelligence on a scale she had never encountered here. She engorged herself with its power, replenishing her depleted energy and immersing herself in a multitude of facts about the present time. Gaining a complete comprehension of this society and its inhabitants would make it much easier to carry out her now complex mission.

       ■   ■   ■

"System crashing!" someone hollered. The cry reverberated in the tech control room amid scrambling, shouts, and stunned faces as flashes of brilliant light pulsed from screens with a dizzying display of rapidly scrolling reams of code.

A minute later, a SWAT team burst in, thudding feet pounding above the din. "Who's the senior security tech on duty?" the team commander demanded. Jeff grumbled to himself as he acknowledged. This could be a long night. "Status?" the commander asked.

"Looks like a cyberattack. Power's being accessed from an unknown source and is being drained at an accelerated rate." Jeff flicked his head at the technicians who had regained their composure and were following the standard protocols. "We're utilizing the built-in anti-intrusion tools to purge any malware left behind and powering down as safely as we can."

       ■   ■   ■

With the enormous amount of energy and data she had tapped into in the server, TuMa'Aye was back on track. Just when she was considering her next move, she sensed an approaching enemy. Whatever it was, it seemed intent on obliterating her. She had to get out quickly. Since online data didn't describe built-in security in the personal terms that she experienced it, she had no way of knowing that was what had been activated against her.

She had ingested so much power there was a good chance the humans would be able to see her rainbow aura. Fortunately, the technicians were so focused on the cyber emergency that no one noticed the fly emerge from the server room and land on a potted plant near the main door. TuMa'Aye had to wait for someone to open the door. She lingered on a leaf until the technical crew determined that the threat was over and no damage had been done; the duty officer called for the previously scheduled shift change.

As Jeff passed by the plant on his way out, he brushed its leaves gently and murmured, "Sorry for the ruckus. I'll water you tomorrow." Lured by the energy of his bond with the plant TuMa'Aye followed him through the door and outside. In the parking lot she changed into a tree frog and attached herself to Jeff's moving machine, a truck. The knowledge she had absorbed from the Internet made almost everything obvious. She had the tools now to easily assume a more authentic human form than ever before and to communicate effectively with people using language. This young technician would be a good start. She just had to conceive a plan he would believe and create a persona that would interest him. No small feat.

After traveling for some time Jeff parked his truck in front of a small, early twentieth century craftsman-style house surrounded with vegetation. He went inside, the door closing behind him. TuMa'Aye waited in a flowerpot on the front porch. A few minutes later he came out with a sandwich and a bottle of beer and sank into the battered rocker beside her. The sense of connection with living things was strong. She studied the way he sat back after he finished eating and gazed at the sky, which was clear and sparkling with stars. A sliver of moon smiled down on them. When Jeff rose and opened the screen door TuMa'Aye hopped inside.

She waited until he fell asleep and released the frog glamour, letting herself revert to her natural state—an amorphous field of barely perceptible energy emitting a scintillating rainbow aura. She went to work reaching into his mind that was open and penetrable in slumber and rounded off her research at his computer where she could glean more data on him. She found a complex mind, highly intelligent, but replete with complicated conflicts and contradictory strands of identity and belief, yet with consistent ethics and reverence for life. TuMa'Aye was convinced that The Living World had led her to Jeff; he was just the person she needed for her new mission. The data she had recently acquired on human anatomy, biological systems, and emotions would allow her to fashion herself into a being resembling a human so closely that only a DNA test could reveal that she wasn't one. The task at hand was to combine the traits that made his colleague Marie, his true but unacknowledged soul mate, with the looks of the perfect fantasy woman she had found clinging to adolescent infatuations rooted in the formation of his personality and masculine identity. Someone he would inexplicably be drawn to. TuMa'Aye would become the "woman of his dreams."

CHAPTER THREE

Tami stretched her human body on the chaise in her Dream Catcher room and assessed the state of her energy. It was odd for a Synon to be feeling drained, but it had taken tremendous amounts of power and concentration to manipulate energy-matter to form this new human persona.

The online profile she had created for herself had been easy to accomplish. For all intents and purposes, she was now a bona fide person with a viable social security number and all the outward trappings. She had been careful to avoid impinging on the data of any real person. However, becoming immersed in this complicated body and managing human interactions could prove a double-edged sword. If she didn't tread carefully she could undermine her mission and her very existence.

In the Realm, there had been persistent rumors about Synons, those dubbed "missing," who were so seduced by their adopted personas that they lost the ability to travel between dimensions and became stuck in the human world. The Realm needed their queen to return unscathed. She had to maintain her essence and not become so immersed that she became this Tami Graves she had created. She seemed to have passed the first test: Jeff Hawke accepted her as Tami Graves, a woman who had clearly had an effect on him.

■   ■   ■

In past times, the Realm was constantly bathed in positive energy emanating through the Passageways from Earth.

As one species evolved beyond others in intelligence it retained a palpable identity as an interdependent part of Nature. While this species developed understanding of how Nature functioned, it began to see itself as superior, and as such, entitled to impose itself on the Earth with steadily increasing destruction and domination. The Earth was dug up and tunneled into, forests were denuded, animal and plant species were plundered and cruelly treated, some rendered extinct.

It became increasingly more burdensome for the Realm to maintain contact with this species, humanity, as it withdrew from Nature. Synons made more frequent visits to Earth, learning how to impersonate people, attempting to understand them. They began to shape their own Realm in the guise of human habitats and even fashioned themselves into human semblances, in effect role-playing in efforts to better comprehend.

Now Tork, second only to TuMa'Aye Gra'Vay in power, sat on a plush circular couch within an undefined space. He wore a dark blue suit, gray silk shirt, and multicolored tie. He appeared to be of middle age, gray-haired, fit. Other Synons were arrayed around him, in varied impersonations of modern sophisticated people.

"Not one of us could have accomplished what TuMa'Aye has. I'm astounded," Tork announced.

A young "woman" called Annilu, also attired in a business suit, spoke shyly. "I have little experience on Earth, yet I find myself distressed by the extremes to which she has gone. Do we no longer have boundaries regarding our invasion of human psyches and manipulating them?"

A babble ensued as those present, practicing their use of physical human speech, expressed their opinions. Judilay, who wore a darker skinned male persona and colorful, casual clothes, interjected. "From what she's relayed to us, the situation on Earth is far worse than we imagined. Perhaps it calls for extreme and innovative action. I, for one, would welcome the opportunity of traveling to assist her."

Tork frowned. "She doesn't need our presence right now. We must allow her to unfold her plan, then assess its effectiveness. I understand the concerns about the lengths to which she's gone. She is called Queen of Realm due to her strength and because of her experience, insight, and accurate decisions. We will monitor her progress." The couch disappeared, leaving the Synons floating within a cloud of weak energy.

*　　*　　*

Jeff Hawke couldn't shake the lingering effect of Tami Graves, like the residue of a dream that persisted long into the day.

His usual intense focus on work wavered during the afternoon as she wafted through his mind. He battled with himself. Knowing that Sarah usually served her guests afternoon refreshments, he fought an overwhelming urge to visit the inn right after his shift. His only reason for doing so would be to see Tami Graves. How long had it been since he had even set foot in the Dream Catcher? Sarah had sounded a bit surprised at his call that afternoon asking about vacancies. The cousins had been close in childhood, but even though living in the same city now, they were more like acquaintances than close friends.

Jeff had told Sarah that he had just happened to meet a young woman who was looking for a place to stay. Would it seem too obvious if he dropped by today? Sarah was perceptive. She would instantly be aware of his interest. Why should he worry? After all, she could also be quite the tease, or worse, the match-maker. He would force himself to wait a day or so. What if by then, Tami was too busy to hang around for wine or tea parties? What if she had already left town? That was a thread to follow. She didn't even live there. What could come of—of what? He felt like slapping his own face. He was acting like an infatuated teen. Go to happy hour after work with the gang. Maybe have some dinner out. Stay in his own world. That's what he'd do.

■　　■　　■

Back in her room, Tami was fully alert and fretting. How was she going to pull off this journalism hoax? Tami felt like she was losing her edge. She had spoken too quickly, grabbing a topic that had impressed itself firmly in her mind after her encounter with the Internet at the police station. She had not weighed her options and planned responses before barging into a conversation with Jeff Hawke in the diner. She had seized upon a crucial topic that should be explored.

She was in an academic, technical, and scientific tri-city area where she had no doubt she could locate viable people to interview. How was she to gain access to them? She had no valid credentials. An idea arose. Maybe she could build on her fabricated identity, giving herself credibility as a writer. No. Things had changed drastically since her last foray into this world. Now, anyone could search out anyone's entire background, easily finding contacts to query in search of verification. Ample evidence would exist for a writer experienced enough to be handed this kind of assignment. She could not bill herself as a book author either. The people she sought to interview should be aware of her books that would logically be in a field of interest to them. If it weren't for her desire to get closer to the Hawke family she could simply abandon the whole scheme.

Tami really needed to learn as much as she could about the astonishing technical advances humans were making. Why hadn't she been informed of this before? Surely Synon visitors had observed this rapid development. A thought struck her: perhaps the Synons who had not returned to the Realm preferred to keep the knowledge unknown. Now humanity was so technically advanced that it was conceivable that in the not-too-distant future they could actually discover the Passageways between the two universes. No human had ever tried to enter the Realm; and since it had always seemed impossible, no Synon thought had ever been given to it. It appeared that the physical matter in which humans were housed could never bridge a Passageway, yet they already understood the principles by which matter and energy were interchangeable.

The data she had ingested told her that scientists were delving into that very phenomenon. Chatter about parallel dimensions and universes permeated the data stream. Should she return to the Realm right away to begin a dialogue on this issue or should she gather more evidence first? Suddenly her initial mission of saving the Passageways seemed ironic. Perhaps human science would discover the Passageways. What would be the consequences? Would The Living World take the extreme step of intervening?

She opened the laptop she had purchased with "money," which she had converted from tree leaves, and connected it to the Wi-Fi, eager to experiment with her newfound knowledge and skills. At least she could research who was working on relevant projects. If she found promising leads she would pursue her original plan. That meant creating a much more complete professional history for Tami Graves.

■ ■ ■

"Her power almost overwhelmed me. I could hardly maintain my own persona." Miriam Jordan lurked in dark shadows within the city arboretum, her appearance ghostly.

George, equally ephemeral, replied, like Miriam, no actual sound emanating, as thoughts drifted between them. "I have never encountered such a powerful Synon. Of course," he said, chuckling, "I haven't sought them out these past decades, hiding out to live like we want to as humans."

Miriam was uncharacteristically assertive. "We should have been more vigilant. Paid more attention to what was happening in the Realm. Our positions here would be compromised if the Realm learned we had defected."

"What could they do?" he interrupted. "The Realm isn't even real. At least in the way Earth is. Synons are just blobs of energy that play around in the Realm creating the illusion of people and their environments to amuse each other. They've mostly made short trips here, and many of those only as observers, cloaked as animals."

"That's not entirely true, George. Many attempted to fulfill our mission, subtly intervening to rebuild human connection to The Living World. That usually requires taking on human personas."

George guffawed. "And those are the ones who realized how much better it is to actually have a life than to imitate one. They stayed." He enjoyed proclaiming his opinions. "Could the Realm force us to return? Suppose we threatened to reveal ourselves to the humans? What would they do then? No, I think we're safe."

Miriam had found her voice as her own convictions rose to the surface. "The price we've paid is ignorance of what has transpired in the Realm."

"All the more reason to continue our work of closing any Passageways not shut down by humanity's defection from Nature. If Synons can't get here, they can't find us and confront us. They would be trapped here." He sneered.

"That will also cut off the possibility of other Synons joining us."

"There are enough of us here already, any one of whom could decide to return to the Realm. Would they be able to keep quiet about how many others reside here as humans? Right now we have to do something about this Tami Graves persona. We know nothing about her. I'm not entirely sure she didn't perceive us despite our efforts to block her."

"The mind blocks we've perfected and the alteration you made to her wine seemed to work."

"Speaking of wine, Miriam, you've acquired too much of a taste for it. You know we can't process alcohol. Beware of its consequences."

"I have no problem with it." She quickly returned to the primary topic. "Should we ask other renegade Synons about her? Do we need to enlist their help?"

"They have varying agendas."

She snapped at him. "Maybe they've found better methods for forming and holding human personas! I'm getting tired of always having to be so concerned that my power will drop and I'll begin to fade right in front of real humans. If other renegades can help us, we should seek them out."

"Let's think carefully about that. We don't really know what their objectives are. Now we have to return to the Dream Catcher for the night."

■ ■ ■

Tami spent the rest of that night building a professional past for herself. It was immensely enjoyable and satisfying.

She felt fused with this computer network people had devised. She planned a busy day. First, she had to make appointments with the scientists who looked most promising. Then she had to produce some professional-looking samples of her "prior work." None of it proved as simple as she had assumed. No human ever answered the scientists' phones. She had to leave voicemails that could only be replied to through the inn's telephone number. That presented a new hurdle. She would have to get one of the ubiquitous mobile communication devices people carried around. They looked so unencumbered but were actually tethered via radio waves to bulky towers owned by various corporations who controlled access for a fee. She would have no trouble accessing the appropriate radio signals to operate it, bypassing the fees and another layer of the ever-present bureaucracy that drove human affairs.

Accomplishing these tasks took the entire day. Moving through the city was slow and tedious. There were no locations sufficiently private to drop and then reform her persona, so she found herself trudging from place to place, waiting at corners for a light to indicate that oncoming vehicles had been ordered to stop so that she could cross, and then vehicles almost collided with her as they turned the same corner in front of her. It seemed incongruous that people had made such advancements in so many areas but moving through a city had changed little more than switching horse-drawn conveyances for automobiles.

Immediately after getting set up with her delightful smart phone, Tami left messages for scientists she hoped to interview. The day passed in a whirl of activity. Her new phone never rang, however. She had called it from her room telephone to make sure it was working properly. It was. At day's end she sat in her room admiring her body of "work." She knew she had committed numerous infractions by fabricating articles by "Tami Graves" in several respected but obscure journals as well as a master of arts thesis from a European university, which she had published in book form. She counted on being able to delete all traces before they were discovered. She was ready to move on if she could just contact someone to interview.

■　　■　　■

Jeff Hawke wielded the pruners as if they were a two-handed sword, taking out his unaccustomed frustration on the recalcitrant branches. Usually the repetition of this task eased him into a Zen-like relaxation, yet today he was unable to enjoy the rare free morning his new shift assignment provided.

He couldn't banish images of Tami Graves, along with a myriad questions about her. He itched to go online to see what was available on her. If she was a journalist there should be records of her prior work. He might also find engagement or wedding announcements. She didn't wear a wedding ring, although some modern couples eschewed that tradition. He forced himself to keep working. He was acting like a silly teenager.

The jangle of his cell phone interrupted the battle in his head. It was Marie from headquarters. She announced that he was summoned to work because the entire system was acting strangely.

"Is that all they can tell me?"

"That's all I can say on an unsecured phone line."

"Whoaa. It's a serious security issue?"

"Chief just says to get in here."

CHAPTER FOUR

Tami had her first interview.

"We're on our way to becoming the Borg." The wild-haired young man grinned, caressing the smart glasses that looked like an eyeglass frame with a small lens just above one eye that could be flipped down. Tami didn't know what he meant. She was afraid it was a term with which she should be familiar, so she just grinned back at him. "You see," he continued, "A.I. machines might evolve separately from us, but the more likely scenario is—oh, excuse me, incoming call. Dr. Frakes here." He rose from his chair and moved out of the office, seemingly talking to the air.

Tami took the opportunity to research "the Borg" on her smart phone and discovered that the term referred to fictional mentally connected cyborgs from a science fiction television show called "Star Trek: The Next Generation" that had first run several decades prior, maintaining popularity through reruns and films available online.

Frakes returned, sliding back into his sleek ergonomic chair.

She almost gloated in displaying her newfound knowledge. "So you think we will merge into a combination of the organic and the technological? And develop a connected hive mentality?" It felt odd to use the term "we."

"We're well on our way." He again caressed his smart glasses. "Are you intrigued by my smart glasses? I developed this model that incorporates everything a mobile phone has and more. This device connects me to the world. There are several forms of wearable technology now. I also have this watch that monitors my vital signs." He waved his arm toward her. "The near future can bring us the same features in implanted form. It almost seems inevitable that we will morph into true cyborgs and perhaps, eventually, shed our fragile organic elements altogether."

Tami's mind was spinning. So much progress so quickly. Were humans getting assistance or was this just their natural mental evolution? How would humanity's relationship with The Living World be affected if it were no longer part of that web of Nature that defined life?

"Dr. Frakes, can you predict a timetable for this evolution?"

"I don't think anyone can; however, at the rate we're progressing, it could be within our lifetime."

"How will we regard Nature if we ourselves are machines?" There. She had said it.

"Well, look what we're doing to the planet already. We're on the road to making it unlivable, anyway. Becoming machines might be the only way we can survive."

"This doesn't appall you?" She didn't have a human digestive system, but she suddenly felt she understood the term "queasy."

"Destroying Nature? Sure. If that's where evolution is taking us. Look, a meteor could hit us and bring on a nuclear winter effect. Any number of things can happen. Plus, the Earth just can't sustain the growing human population as is. If we didn't need food and water we'd be much better off. That factor alone could alleviate a great deal of conflict."

"What about the unique animal and plant life?"

He seemed irritated. "I don't know. Maybe we'd want to preserve specimens. Maybe we just wouldn't care. That's an issue for others to consider."

"Do you know anyone who is? Could you put me in touch?"

■　　■　　■

Jeff found headquarters on a high-alert level. An untraceable hacker was attempting to gain control of the computer system.

"Do you think this is related to the power drain incident the other day?" The chief marched around the conference table at which sat precinct captains and several of their top computer people; he looked right at Jeff.

"Its signature is different, but the process is similar. However, this goes way beyond that incident," Jeff replied. "In that event there was no apparent attempt to gain control like this."

"Doesn't it seem strange that two incidents hap—" The chief's phone interrupted. He answered and listened a few moments, gave a terse response and disconnected. He turned to the group, "The mayor is taking measures. Meantime, we need to stay on it. Any theories?"

"First thought is obviously terrorism. Why a city police department?" No one was surprised that a lieutenant in charge of cyber-crime piped up first suggesting terrorism.

A captain jumped in. "Is it just a local threat? Maybe it's organized crime trying to send us a message."

"Maybe they're just testing their ability to see how far they can reach and maintain control. The plan could be to expand." Marie, Jeff's colleague, was the only woman in the room. Her voice sounded oddly high-pitched after the almost growling vocal styles just heard, and her small frame and delicate beauty gave her a childlike appearance at the huge table among a group of burly men.

The chief did not respond to Marie, again looked to Jeff. "Who would have this kind of capability?"

Jeff felt uncomfortable. He didn't like getting into specifics this early. There was no evidence yet. He hedged. "They disabled our firewalls and anti-intrusion systems. Our recent work toward a more integrated city-wide system has me worried. It won't take them long to get into other municipal departments. Going beyond the city system will require them to start all over again learning to disable new security protocols. If they try it, I think that might give us a little time." He hadn't meant to say so much. He was thinking out loud. He felt even more uncomfortable than before.

"Excellent assessment." Chief Freeman looked as if he might pat Jeff on the back. "Everybody get on this. Dig for any connection that your specialization might have. Cyber Terrorism, work with IT in each precinct, get people looking for who might be out there. Something Jeff said about city departments stuck out. They could get into the city's financial system. Maybe that's the objective. An old-fashioned robbery. Keep each other and me informed. And, until it gets out to the public, keep it "need to know". Let's go to it." A half-smile flashed across his face as he strode out the door.

■　■　■

Jeff's concentration was broken by the buzzing of his cell phone lying next to the computer. He glanced at it and was surprised to see the name Tami Graves flashing next to an unfamiliar phone number.

He was torn. No way should he take a personal call in the middle of this crisis; neither could he stop himself from answering. He swiftly donned the ear bud and microphone. "Hello, Tami. I see you got a phone with a local number." He hoped that sounded casual but interested.

"Yes. I might be staying here a while. My research is taking several fascinating directions, which leads to why I called you."

Business. He felt a pungent disappointment. "How can I help you?" He tried to sound detached.

"Did I get you at an awkward time? You sound a bit distracted."

"There's been an incursion into our network. I can only talk a minute."

"That sounds bad. I won't keep you. I'm told that you're active in a conservation movement called the Living World."

"Uh, yeah, when I have time I help them out."

"Jeff, I'm just curious. Do you know how that name originated?"

"Sure. I'm actually one of the early members. We were trying to think of a name. One day the founder, who happened to be my uncle, came to a meeting saying that he had dreamed a name. The Living World. We all liked it and so it was adopted."

"Is this the same uncle who originally owned the Dream Catcher?"

"Yeah, it was. Ironic. He hankered to get off the reservation. Well, that's what some of us kids called it, like movies, but when he got immersed in city life he became a crusader for protecting Nature, again, just like the stock image of Indians. What's your interest in all this?"

"I guess mostly the attitude I'm getting from sci—."

■   ■   ■

There was an audible gasp from Jeff. "Gotta go, Tami." He disconnected as he spoke.

Strange code was coursing on his screen, too rapid to read. He heard gasps and exclamations around him as colleagues realized that the entire municipal system code had been hijacked and was being rewritten.

Jeff's perception of and reaction to the system takeover was instantaneously communicated to Tami even as he abruptly disconnected. It overshadowed the wonderful surprise in the story Jeff had told her just before hanging up. Was it serendipity that Jeff and his uncle had formed a group they called the Living World? Even more relevant was the revelation that Jeff's uncle had dreamed the name. Could The Living World have implanted the name in his dream? If so, that could mean this was all part of a larger plan and that she had been destined to meet the Hawke family.

Jeff was fascinating. Her foray into his mind had offered insights into his personality that might be hidden to his conscious mind. It was the deepest she had ever delved into a human's psyche, and she felt a responsibility to protect his privacy and never allow him to know what she had done. His sense of violation and being laid open to another in such a manner would certainly threaten any positive relationship between them. She must be careful. He was strong yet emotionally fragile. She knew that he was attracted to the Tami Graves persona. She needed to build a friendship and trust between them while deflecting any romantic tinges engendered by the feelings evoked by the female appearance she had blithely plucked from his adolescent memories, ignorant of the persistence of its evocative power. She wished she more fully understood the complexities of human emotional relationships.

■   ■   ■

Tami sat at a table outside a café within a university complex, a place of respite surrounded by busy activity.

She couldn't shake the vivid telepathic message that had been carried by the telephone link. Someone had the capability to break into and control the secure municipal computer network. She wanted to help Jeff. What could she do? Abruptly, Tami knew what she had to do. She surveyed the buildings around her. One stood out. Engraved across its ornate front was the word "Library."

A sudden compulsion overtook her, propelling her toward the building. Then reason ascended, compelling her to stop short of the wide, steep expanse of stairs. She needed to be a fly again. Could she contain her vast store of energy in the body of such a tiny creature now? Could she regain the glamour after she performed her intended actions? Would she be able to maintain it long enough to reclaim the Tami Graves persona? She had to make the effort. The need for seclusion made her look around quickly to see if anyone was nearby who might notice her; she saw only a few people lost in their own thoughts or using electronic devices. Mature trees shaded the entire area, and precisely manicured bushes lined the walkway and either side of the stairs, with no safe place to transition. Would there be somewhere inside? With determination, she strode up the stairs.

Once inside Tami studied the directory and found the perfect place. She followed arrows to the alcove above which was emblazoned the word "Restrooms." She laughed to herself: You've just got to start thinking more like a woman. She was forced to wait inside a stall for what seemed an interminably long time as women continuously came and went, each seeming to take longer than the prior. Finally, she heard no movement and sensed no presence. In a few minutes, a common fly hovered, now impatiently wishing the horde of women who had just passed through would return and open the door to the hall. Eventually, she was free. Now she had to wait for other doors to open as she searched for the computer servers. A ravishing hunger seized her, and she had to force herself to tamp down the anticipation of a new encounter with this wondrous Internet humans had devised.

When she had accomplished her goal of entering the Internet, the experience was satiating, yet left her wistful. The freedom of frolicking in her pure form without the drudgery of maintaining a human persona was intoxicating. TuMa'Aye

Gra'Vay soaked up raw knowledge and was thrilled by the resultant electrifying associations and revelations. Comprehension flooded her awareness. These poor humans had advanced technologically far beyond their emotional and cultural maturity; still, they clung to superstition. A dangerous situation.

This sobering realization brought TuMa'Aye back to her objective. She focused, homing in on the local municipal, then the police network, cautiously examining it in tiny increments for any hint of malevolent presence. She found busy chaos amid frantic activity from many sources.

TuMa'Aye Gra'Vay reached out searching for any strand she could find that might indicate the presence of intruders. What she felt was startling: distinctive Synon energy infused with aggression and malice. The invaders were Synons! The shock diminished her focus to the point that her essence wavered, nearly dissipating beyond cohesion. Violence among Synons was unknown. Her missions through Passageways had always been peaceful. Even though those missions often focused on helping people resolve conflicts, she had carefully avoided involvement in physical confrontations. She didn't know how to fight.

Abruptly, an onslaught of concentrated energy struck her with such force that it literally propelled her backward, followed by smaller, intense bursts. The attack came from all directions, keeping her in stasis. A stronger barrage of energy slammed into her, turning her attention to simple survival. Her only option was to fight back. Instinct took over, perhaps honed by the past human battles she had sadly witnessed. She unleashed a small portion of her vast energy reserve, hurling it in the direction of the last volley against her. That brought even more focused bursts that violently pummeled her, again putting her on the defensive. Then renewed attacks from other directions, although weaker, combined to surround her.

Synons obviously controlled the network where she was. They could destroy her. They should know that they had attacked another Synon. Did they recognize her? What kind of transformation had been necessary for them to function so effectively in this alien environment? Had they given up some of the essence that made them Synons? They obviously knew that a strong energy force confronted them; perhaps she was unidentifiable to them, simply an intruder.

Then disruptive action sifted through the barrier surrounding her. It started slowly eating away at the enemy area right behind her. She cautiously joined the effort and was accepted by whoever it was. Ever so slowly this combined force bore through the Synon barricade, enabling her to backtrack to her entry point. Just before exiting, TuMa'Aye extended her awareness sending the image of a hand reaching out in gratitude. A return image clearly showed her a man's hand reaching for her own. A beaded ring brought a rush of recognition. It was the hand of Jeff Hawke.

■   ■   ■

Stunned, Jeff Hawke stared at his computer screen trying to make sense of what he had just experienced while trying to decipher just who or what had seized the municipal computer system.

He had encountered what was clearly two opposing forces. One of them was so powerful that it had surrounded the other and was about to annihilate it. An intuitive urge to aid the weaker force impelled him into the fray, instinctively manipulating the digital environment to distract the attacker. Who or what was it? Obviously, he could have encountered any of the other city IT personnel who were working in the system and could have been in trouble. He had perceived a mental vision of a female hand reaching for him that was so compelling it produced a corresponding response from him. He saw his own hand reach out and nearly touch the other. More astonishingly, the presence felt familiar.

He vigorously shook his head, attempting to clear it. He had to focus on what he had observed in a rational way. The feeling persisted that he had witnessed a directed confrontation between sentient entities. He could not use this term with colleagues. Jeff tried to recall the entire experience, and it only reinforced his initial feelings. He had discovered what appeared to be multiple energy sources that were attacking a lone presence, which itself exuded extraordinarily resistant force but was no match for the opposition. Had he not intervened just when he did, Jeff thought that this lone source would have been destroyed. He could not eradicate the notion that he had witnessed a battle between sentient entities and that those who had attacked were the original intruders. Was this lone entity also trying to oust them? It all seemed too unbelievable.

Adding to his confusion was the lingering sensation of familiarity, even a bond, between the lone entity and himself.

"You find something?" Marie was looking at him oddly. "You look like you're in a trance."

"Oh...uh." Jeff blinked and shook his head again. "Maybe. I need to keep working at it. Not sure. I might have just bumped into somebody else."

"You mean somebody else like me, another IT grunt?" Marie cocked one eyebrow.

"Yeah." He turned back to his screen and tried to look like he was concentrating. He couldn't deal with her curiosity right then. It brought him back to reality and the fact that nothing had changed as far as eradicating the invasive software. If the strangely familiar presence had been trying to help, all he had done was assist in its retreat and exit without being destroyed. Perhaps that was one small accomplishment.

■   ■   ■

Tami sat in a library study cubicle. Her strength and focus were gradually returning after reforming her human persona.

She had just been through the most terrifying and simultaneously most fulfilling experience of her long lifetime. She tried to sort out the various elements of her network encounters. One, before the attack, she had ingested a startling amount of amazing and valuable knowledge that gave her detailed and expansive information and understanding about the current state of human civilization on Earth. Two, there was a Synon presence. Three, it was astonishingly strong and aggressive. It had to be multiple Synons working together. Four, she had to assume that these Synons had gained as much knowledge as she had, probably more, giving them an advantage in devising tactics against her and humans. Five, she and Jeff Hawke had met in a revelatory moment that had shown her the meaning of the human word "euphoria." It was a union with another entity unlike any she had ever known and more confusing because it was a human—a specific one with whom she was intrinsically linked. It was almost as if they had shared the most intimate of moments. A new and unique bond was forming that was both troubling and thrilling. Six, she wondered if he had felt it too, and if so, how he had reacted. Was he confused, curious, frightened? Probably all of these and more. People had evolved such a wide array of emotions, which often were in conflict. The more she learned about humans, the more this unique tumult of feelings that characterized them seeped into her. She fully understood how rumored renegade Synons had literally come to regard themselves as so human that they couldn't fathom the idea of returning to the Realm.

That was what was so odd about the Synon cyber intruders. It raised frightening questions about their intentions and capabilities. If this new worldwide connectivity and knowledge source had so infatuated her it could mean that all Synons were susceptible to its lure and the potential for absolute fusion without the encumbrance of physical personas. These cyber-Synons had moved beyond the fascination with impersonating individual humans to becoming a new cyber life-form.

The lurking mystery of closing Passageways, missing Synons, and the absence of reports to the Realm on the speed of human progress now became clearer, with dire meaning. Her strength, strong connectivity, and many trips to Earth had earned TuMa'Aye Gra'Vay the nickname "Queen of the Realm." Although the Realm was without a power structure or government, TuMa'Aye Gra'Vay was acknowledged as its leader and therefore bore some responsibility. She should have been more concerned with the persistent reports of Synons never returning to the Realm from Earth. It had always been attributed to the Passageways closing, which was blamed on human disconnection from The Living World. She had put little credence in the whispers that Synon visitors chose to remain. Some were possibly closing Passageways in an attempt to hinder Synon investigation of them. There could be many of them everywhere.

She looked around her, resisting the urge to invade the psychic privacy of those around her, searching for them. If Synons were here she should sense them, and it was likely they would be aware of her; it was possible that they had developed sophisticated psychic blocks. The persona she was developing was gradually forming human emotions like a brain's neural networks. They surfaced, generating a palpable sense of vulnerability with which she was totally unfamiliar. She tried to shake it off, even as she admitted to herself that her true adversary appeared to be her own kind.

Her mind drifted back to Jeff Hawke. Should she take the tremendous risk of revealing herself to him and telling him about the true nature of the intruders? Would he believe it? Even if he did believe her, could he accept the truth? He might possibly be able to see the intruders as alien or manmade entities. It would take much more to convince him that the beautiful woman to whom he was attracted was one of them. She needed more time to prepare him. How? He was now totally immersed in fighting this invasion. She needed to find a subtle way to help him.

■　　■　　■

The Realm was in a tumult. Its normally pastel tinges vibrated vivid reds and blacks. Some Synons were having difficulty holding their own essences together.

Tork called a conclave. He fashioned a serene green hill with a gentle slope and a blue sky above it. He knew it was imperative, yet even for him it was difficult to form and hold a human persona right then. He chose a historical figure with long white hair and beard wearing a gray robe. He raised his arms to the erratic sea of energy surrounding him. "We are love but are not beings dominated by emotion like humans. Why are you mimicking human panic? These extreme circumstances demand composed reason." He saw efforts within the quivering mass to follow his lead. Some even formed faint human personas. Tork continued. "It is a distressing shock that our kind could do what the queen has uncovered and experienced. I know that only the strongest few among us were able to experience it through her, and I decry those who indiscriminately shared it. However, now that we all are aware we must calmly assess the situation. First, how have we not been aware of what appears to be many Synons who have not returned from missions or made reports? We must hope that only a small number have gone to the abhorrent extremes witnessed. It seems we should emulate our human charges in a way we haven't—their penchant for record keeping. Since we don't see ourselves as discrete identities other than when we role play as humans, we simply do not know how many individual Synons are living on Earth."

A strong voice rang out. "I seem to recall one among us identifying as an archivist, with a goal of maintaining human style records of our progress. Is that archivist present?" The only reply was a buzz of energy from the gathering. No voice emerged.

Tork said, "I now recall the same. Where and how was this archive to have been established? It would take enormous power to maintain it in a facsimile of permanent matter."

The Synon who had first mentioned the archivist replied, "Perhaps the archive was established on Earth and the archivist is there, tending it."

"No." A Synon wearing a tall, male persona strode toward the hill's crest where Tork stood. "I remember him. He flitted around here with an officious manner."

Tork retook control. "It matters not. He isn't here to provide information. We must act now. It is imperative for us to gather positive energy and send it to our queen to remind her of our support. She is in the best position now to ascertain the ways in which Synons are behaving on Earth and what their impact is. She will know we are ready to provide whatever she needs."

    ▪   ▪   ▪

Sitting in the library cubicle, mind in a whirl and assailed with unfamiliar feelings, TuMa'Aye felt herself transported to a green hilltop beneath a blue sky. Positive energy enveloped her. She felt its peace and strength flow through her. It would guide her.

CHAPTER FIVE

"Take a break, Jeff. Get some dinner. You need a little downtime to be at your best," his watch commander insisted.

Jeff could use a break. He was on edge and operating on adrenalin. He had been ignoring his growling stomach. A nice meal seemed extremely inviting. An idea popped into his head and without stopping to consider his actions he took out his cell and called Tami Graves.

She answered immediately. "Hello, Jeff. Are you all right?"

Why would she ask him that? "Sure," he replied, puzzled. "A little tired and a lot hungry and just ordered to go out and get some dinner. Could you join me?"

"I'd love to. I'm at the university library and can meet you pretty quickly. You pick a convenient place."

■　■　■

They settled on a cozy Italian bistro and in twenty minutes were sitting across from each other, but conversation didn't come easily.

Tami had arrived first, and when she saw him approaching her she felt a sudden warmth gush over her and knew that her face had reddened with what people called blushing. She managed to control the response. When he reached her, he smiled and touched her shoulder, eliciting the blushing anew, along with a strange tingling that seemed to make her body shiver. She had learned nuances of human emotion and was translating that knowledge into physical responses and behavior totally without control. With heightened awareness she felt uneasy shyness in Jeff, mingled with the same sense of elation she had felt when their hands touched in cyberspace. As they grinned at each other she saw their auras softly meshing, and she shrugged it all off as compatible aural frequencies. She admonished herself: relax, you're just experiencing how the physical world works.

■　　■　　■

Once they were seated, perusing the menu and ordering consumed a bit of the awkward silence. As they waited for the food Jeff broke the ice. He had regained some composure after his surprising bashfulness at unconsciously touching Tami's shoulder. He tried to make small talk, genuinely interested in learning more about her. "Where are you from originally? How do you like it here?"

She hesitated a moment. "I had a…let's simply call it bad… childhood that I have worked through but now prefer to forget and not discuss at all. On a brighter note, I really like it here and want to explore the rest of the state, especially the mountains. Did you grow up in Cherokee?"

Now it was Jeff who hesitated. He felt a bit hurt that she was shutting him out from any explanation of her past life, but he had the same reluctance to discuss his own. "Yeah. I left, went to college, then joined the military. Got into IT and wound up here."

"You had some family here."

"Yeah, my uncle and cousin."

"Do you have other family? Wife? Children?"

That line of questioning threw him and he stammered, grinning. "Naw...you?"

"Still single. Guess I'm a career girl all the way."

"Well some women combine both." He felt silly. That was a stupid retort.

"Maybe someday. Now I'm just enjoying myself. Do you ever visit Cherokee? I'd love a personal tour."

"Don't get back much. Work is busy, and shifts change frequently." He didn't know how to answer the invitation for a personal tour. He didn't want to let her know that he was not on the best of terms with those he'd left behind, yet he felt compelled to reveal some of it. "I guess I was like most kids—rebel against your own situation. Anyway, now I see that I became too outspoken about my feelings and probably hurt some people that I really cared about."

"Your feelings about what?"

"Uh, being an Indian. My family was very traditional and tried to push it off on me. I didn't want any part of it. Wanted to get out. You know, like kids do."

"Did your feelings change as you matured?"

"Sort of. When I got back in touch with my uncle, especially. I guess I just couldn't purge myself of all the things other people connect with being Indian, like the stereotyped love of Nature and wanting to preserve it. I was sort of reluctant at first to get involved in my uncle's Nature organization; now I'm glad I did. People have too much of an attitude that they're above everything else on the Earth. We're not. We're part of a whole." He felt a bit sheepish, as if he'd gotten on a soapbox and made a speech, confirming the stereotype.

"Reverence for Nature is embedded in humans. Modern industrialized and urbanized society has just buried it very deeply. There seems to be a global return to conservation, in part driven by science in reaction to the looming climate crisis."

He wanted to change the subject. Talking about work took him back into his own world and some sense of control, even though he found himself saying things he hadn't planned to articulate to anyone. "I had a strange experience online today. I don't know how much of it I should reveal because of security, but I know you're interested in, uh, theoretical science." He rushed right into the topic. "Our municipal network has been invaded with the strongest malware I've ever seen or heard of. It's almost totally taken control, and if that happens, it could branch out to other networks we're linked to, which could become a catastrophe of cascading proportions."

"I do know a bit about computer science. It sounds like it has a pervasive aspect. Is it broken down into components?"

"Yes," he answered eagerly, leaning toward her. "It could be self-replicating. It seems like much more than software. I got a weird feeling today of multiple, uh, I want to say sentient entities; I know that sounds crazy and has to be inaccurate."

"Why?" She also leaned forward, their foreheads almost touching. "We often think of an entity as something alive, but is it necessarily sentient or self-aware? Nanobots that can self-replicate already exist. The goal of artificial intelligence is to create independent thinking machines that can make decisions, take actions, learn, and self-replicate. It sounds like someone has done this and is testing it on your network."

Jeff sighed. "I'm so glad you don't think I'm crazy. There's more, even—" He paused as the waiter arrived and served their salads. "—even weirder." He looked down at his plate and picked up his fork; when he looked up again saw the interest in Tami's eyes as she sat looking intently at him, ignoring her food. "I had a distinct impression that the entities were in conflict, with one group literally ganged up on a lone entity and trying to drive it out." He took a bite of salad, waiting for her response. He didn't know why he had told her all of that. Her intent gaze had seemed to mesmerize him.

She continued to ignore the food in front of her, apparently engrossed in thought. "So more than one person or group has perfected this technology and are battling it out for dominance. Divide and conquer." She seemed to realize that food was before her and took a small bite, still watching him.

"That makes sense. Rivals who might have even been colleagues and are now in competition. Winner take all. Maybe the biggest prize ever."

Tami looked like the clichéd lightbulb had just lit up above her head. "Maybe we're jumping to conclusions, just looking at what we are most familiar with." She paused as if reaching for the right words. "Now you might think I'm the crazy one. But. But, what if they are sentient entities and not manmade technology?"

He interrupted, eyes wide, "You mean like aliens?"

"I do." She looked serious.

He pushed back unruly dark hair falling near his eyes and didn't miss a beat in the conversation. "Nothing should be ruled out at this stage. Most scientists seem to be certain that there is other life beyond Earth, and it could take any form. If we can rationally discuss the kind of entities I've described being products of human engineering, then certainly another civilization could have developed them along with the means to inject them into our cyberspace." He paused, with a puzzled expression. "Why pick only one city to invade and why this one? We're not a major national or international player."

"Testing. Practicing. Perhaps some factors we wouldn't even think of made this a target." She didn't seem the least bit disturbed by the prospect they so rationally discussed. She was amazing. Most women would either be howling in laughter or howling with hysteria.

■   ■   ■

Tami had been relieved when Jeff turned the conversation toward the cyberattack.

Her developing human emotions were making her feel manipulative and deceitful by mentally nudging Jeff to talk about himself. She was still subtly trying to influence him, albeit on a matter of dire importance. She had found a way to bring to the discussion a version of what she knew was the truth and Jeff had accepted the possibility. Then he backtracked.

Jeff chuckled. "I guess we have the same kind of wild imagination. There's a logical explanation for 'why here.' We're in a high-tech center. If someone were going to make this breakthrough in artificial intelligence they could certainly be here.

And that would explain the incursion into the convenient municipal network, as you said, for testing."

Tami grappled for a way to discredit this all too feasible theory and steer Jeff back to the "unknown alien" notion. Jeff stayed on target. "It could be some of the very people you've been researching, Tami. You might already have significant leads."

"The people I'm looking at are working in different areas of AI, more human-like robotics. I can't think of any one of them who would be capable of this."

"The more I think about it, the more I realize I have to take this idea upstairs. Even if they laugh at me, I'm obligated to report anything unusual I find."

Tami seized on that line of reasoning. "It seems the right thing to do. You need to compare notes with others anyway. Someone else might have encountered these entities as well."

Their entrees had arrived and barely been touched. Jeff abruptly dug into his. "I'd better take advantage of this opportunity for some good food. When I go in with this, I'll probably be shunted between bureaucrats and security brass. Once we part ways after dinner, don't be surprised if we can't communicate."

"I'll do what research I can. Hopefully, if I come up with something there will be some way to contact you."

"Don't count on it unless you have high security clearance."

Tami felt a tug of anguish. The bond between them went beyond closed doors and unanswered phones. She longed to make him aware of it, knowing all the while that she was experiencing illogical impulses. The memory of their avatar hands touching flared into her awareness. She had been waiting for him to make some mention of it when he had spoken of his weird experience and was disappointed when he did not. With no conscious plan or intent, she sent the image and the emotions it stirred in her to Jeff.

She saw him shiver, clinch his eyes shut, and grip the napkin in his hand so tightly it would have ripped if it had been paper instead of cloth. He sighed loudly, then shook his head vigorously, dark hair flying. His eyes flew open, but he didn't release his grip on the napkin. He stared at her.

Tami knew instantly that she had made a mistake. She hoped her startled look was realistic. "Jeff! What's wrong?" Her voice was tinged with alarm, not all of it subterfuge.

He just kept shaking his head. "I don't know. I really don't. I think maybe they," he hesitated, hand again plowing through his hair. "I think they implanted an image in my mind. Maybe trying to throw me off."

"What kind of image?"

"Hands. One of them definitely mine. The other reaching for me."

Tami had regained strategic thinking. "Didn't you say that one of these entities was being attacked by others? It's not inconceivable that it would be able to project this image to you. Maybe it was pleading for help."

"There was an element of need and fear; the overwhelming sensation I felt was—" He blew his breath out through his mouth, hand again raking hair. "I felt a wave, no, a current, of connection. I can't explain it. It must have been a hallucination-type thing from concentrating so intently and for so long."

"Maybe you're underestimating these entities. Perhaps they are more than machines." A surge of joy had coursed through her at his revelation. It was difficult to focus on the task at hand.

He growled. "Or maybe they're machines that can get into our minds and manipulate them."

Time to reinforce her suggestion. "And maybe they are both machine and sentient, telepathic entities. Or entities that can somehow, I don't know…" She shrugged, throwing up her hands as if in frustration. "…I'm just thinking out loud, brainstorming, uh, maybe they can change form."

"Like shape-shifters in sci-fi?" He blew out breath again in a skeptical laugh. Then cocked an eyebrow. "You know, there are shape-shifters in a lot of ancient folklore and mythologies. Sci-fi writers didn't invent the idea."

She took up the thread. "There's conjecture that ancient myth and art depicting certain beings and phenomena are based on actual alien sightings and even interactions."

He laughed, humming the *Twilight Zone* theme song. She joined him, surprised at the extent of her popular culture knowledge and relieved that she had deflected his thinking.

"I can't suggest stuff like that to the brass. I think I just won't mention the hand image." He was more relaxed now. "I don't want to, anyway. Whatever it was, it just felt like a special moment between me and whatever that was. When that image just now flashed in my head again I felt happier than I ever have. More than happiness, it was like a feeling of oneness with…" more head shaking and hair raking, then a small laugh almost like a childish giggle. "…The Force. It was like The Force was with me." His next laugh was robust and jocular. "That sounds like a major drug trip." A sour look crept across his face. "Whatever that thing was, it's messing with my mind big time. I don't like that. Not one bit." Jeff's entire demeanor had changed.

He spit out the last words through clenched teeth, sitting up straight, hands braced against the table.

Tami flinched. Her euphoria at his confession about his experience vanished. This was the wrong outcome. How could people switch attitudes so rapidly? She tried to soften his mood. "You can't know that. The one that sent you the hand image could have been trying to soothe you. It could have been, to continue the metaphor, the Light Side of the Force."

"And Darth Vader was attacking it?" He snorted derisively. "Time to get real." He shoveled food into his mouth, mumbling as he chewed. "Do me one favor, Tami."

"Sure." She wondered if this persona she had woven could really cry as she felt was about to happen.

"Forget this conversation about the phantom cyber hands. I think we feed each other's imaginations a lot of craziness. I can't risk my credibility at work." He signaled the waiter for the check. "My treat, and I can't say it hasn't been fascinating." He was already on his feet, throwing cash on the table. "It's kind of late now. Can you get back to the B & B okay?"

Awash in a perplexing torrent of emotions, she found herself replying in a bitter tone, unable to look at him. "I can take care of myself." He stalked away, leaving her sitting there trying to cope with what was happening to her. Hurt. She was hurt by his sudden change in demeanor. Loss. She feared she had lost his friendship and trust. Confusion. What was going on with her? These unfamiliar feelings were clouding her usually clear thinking. Fear. Suppose she was losing her ability to control her persona and its behavior?

Tami went outside and walked, questions swirling. Paramount was why she was becoming so emotional. She had only been here a few days. In past missions she had stayed longer, mingling with people. She had always been able to remain aloof, not actually getting tangled up in human relationships. Maybe she was fooling herself, like people did. Perhaps in the past she had buried feelings and not allowed herself to remember them. Maybe the experiences had a cumulative effect. She had sparked deep feelings within Jeff Hawke. It was only natural that reciprocal emotions would seep through his bond to her. And certainly, she had never before attempted to deliberately gain a human man's affection. She had to admit that was exactly what she was doing. She was playing with Jeff Hawke. She had stolen his innermost secrets and made them live. By human standards she was despicable. He didn't know what she'd done, so this guilt and feeling of having perpetrated a heinous betrayal did not come from him. It was within her.

Was this happening to the missing Synons? If she experienced such drastic change in just a few days how were they coping with longer exposure? Maybe they avoided close relationships with humans and formed their own communities. How many Synons were here? Were any still working toward their core mission? The cyber intrusion clearly demonstrated that some Synons had, indeed, taken on the worst of human attributes.

It suddenly hit her that her efforts to sway Jeff toward the truth about the intruders could have little benefit. It didn't provide a solution. Could even the most skilled computer experts confront the Synons within the network? Alone, she had almost been destroyed by them. Only stronger Synon intervention could have any effect. Should she return to the Realm? No. This was an immediate danger and she needed to enlist the help of

Synons already here. She had to focus on her search for them. She thought of the strange couple at the Dream Catcher. She had suspicions about them. If they were Synons they had developed mental barriers. However, they would have been able to read her and recognize that she was one of their kind. They had made no attempt to communicate this to her, so she had to assume that they wanted to maintain their secret identities. She decided to try getting them alone the next day. She would have to find a way to approach them. They were her first potential link to other Synons here, other than those who had attacked the city computer network. She had to get past the tangle of her relationship with Jeff and focus on the objectives.

CHAPTER SIX

Miriam and George Jordan nestled within their arboretum hideaway, letting go of the last strands of energy and tension that manifested their physical forms.

Relief washed over them. Despite their embrace of life in the human world, they lacked human bodies and needed the restorative calm that was Synon sleep that now claimed them. The music of crickets and the scent of roses drifted away along with their corporeal bodies. The physical world barely existed.

A rush of energy suddenly slammed into them, almost engulfing their very beings. Their awareness was assaulted by harsh telepathic threats that mocked the human speech they had utilized for so long. "Did you think you could keep us from knowing TuMa'Aye Gra'Vay was here? Why didn't you notify us immediately of her presence and location?" Hostility hovered in the air.

Miriam and George struggled to psychically cling to each other, trying not to be absorbed within the threatening onslaught. The renegade Synon swarm surrounding them plucked from their awareness everything the two had discovered about TuMa'Aye Gra'Vay's presence.

George tried to appease them with excuses. "Is that who the woman at the Dream Catcher is? We knew she was a strong Synon; it never occurred to us that she was the queen herself."

A derisive snort interrupted. "Queen? That's just a nickname. Yes. She is extremely strong and for that reason we should have been notified of her presence."

"We weren't sure how to find you."

One renegade's voice dominated. "Well, I found you, didn't I? Look at you. Puny, pitiful excuses for Synons. You have made yourselves so much in the human image that you give your personas the appearance of age. We should send you back to the Realm, but you would tattle like human children, raising alarms about our actions and intentions here. We need no more meddling visitors from the Realm to absorb. And that's what would happen to any Synon excursions vainly attempting to stop us."

The two Synons who for decades had lived as Miriam and George Jordan were fading, fighting with what strength and autonomy remained to them. George protested, "We have no idea what your intentions are here. We assumed you wanted to live among people and experience the joys of life as they do."

The renegade reveled in the mimic of human speech. "Why would we want to be like inferior beings? We can do so much more, especially by absorbing their energy-matter to strengthen ourselves."

Miriam's shock gave her momentary strength. "You would defile The Living World with such abhorrent action?"

"You are as small-minded as the humans you impersonate, and that makes you dangerous to us."

"I sense the nature of your plan," George's faint mind interjected. "It is atrocious, destructive to The Living World."

"No more so than the humans. We are simply doing now what they are foolishly stumbling toward all too quickly. They would be unequipped to handle the consequences. We, on the other hand, are perfectly fitted to mold this technology-dominated future."

Miriam murmured weakly, "You cannot succeed. The Living World will…" Her existence dissolved. George and Miriam Jordan were no more.

"So unsatisfying." The renegade sighed. "Maybe this TuMa'Aye Gra'Vay will be a little meatier." A raucous laugh reverberated through the arboretum. "Time for us to get back to my new cyber home. The minions I left in charge won't be able to control it for long without me. One more task first."

◾ ◾ ◾

When Tami reached the Dream Catcher it was dark except for the porch lights.

She was still in a turmoil over the outcome of her dinner with Jeff. She strolled behind the inn to the tranquil pond. The streetlamps and inn's exterior lights were too far away to reach this spot. It was dark except for a few stars. Fireflies twinkled around her. The lure of dropping what was now becoming a burdensome human body tugged at her. Why not? No people were around. She stepped into the cool, placid water. She reveled in the tranquil energy flowing through her and let her true essence emerge. There was a surprising amount of positive energy around her. Even though within a bustling city, this particular place was close to The Living World.

The tranquil silence was rent by howling and barking. Something had disturbed the neighborhood dogs. Lights went dark. TuMa'Aye Gra'Vay felt the same threatening presence she had barely escaped while in the computer network. Was it the same Synons or others? Whoever they were, it was clear that they were targeting her. She summoned all her power, reaching out to the natural life around her for support.

"Where is your retinue now, phony queen?" a fabricated male human voice resounded.

"Who are you? What do you want?" she responded. An evil force surrounded her and she knew she faced more than the one entity who spoke.

"You'll know that in a few minutes when I absorb you. Then my power will be so great that no one can touch me, not even the Realm."

TuMa'Aye Gra'Vay lashed out. She knew she was no match for all these Synons and had to find a way out. This time there would be no helping hand from Jeff Hawke. She focused on the one who seemed to be the leader. Sparks of energy lit the darkness like lightning as the two locked in battle. Her tactic proved right; the other Synons hung back, letting the leader control the fight. If she could defeat him perhaps they would be reluctant to tangle with her. Her prior cyber encounter was her only combat experience. It was repugnant to her, yet she knew she had to survive. The renegade leader was strong but was not an adept fighter. He seemed to have no strategy, simply pounding her with as much energy as he could muster in each blast. In contrast, she applied with finesse the vast knowledge of warfare she had gleaned from the Internet. She paced herself, waiting for the slight pauses between his volleys to counterattack. She was the stronger of the two and needed to goad him to deplete his store of energy.

As the conflict raged on new force was building around TuMa'Aye Gra'Vay. The pond's placid water rose up in a whirlpool surrounding her. The trees bent forward, their massive limbs sweeping at the renegades. The gentle breeze was now a torrent of wind ripping through her enemy. Sounds of the stirring neighborhood drifted on the wind, as people ventured outside to discuss the power outage. The din of canine voices continued. People shouted as the pets they attempted to leisurely walk bounded toward the pond. The renegade leader wavered momentarily. TuMa'Aye Gra'Vay struck with potent force as Sarah Hawke stepped out onto her back porch, calling to the group of people and dogs running through her yard. Struggling to maintain his integrity, the renegade leader disengaged and weakly retreated, his followers straggling behind him. The natural onslaught diminished and the neighborhood lights blinked on.

TuMa'Aye Gra'Vay took refuge in the trees giving thanks to the natural forces that had come to her aid.

The dogs were quieting down, and neighbors murmured softly as they gingerly approached the pond that now lay placid among still greenery. TuMa'Aye Gra'Vay moved as close to the sidewalk as seemed safe and reclaimed her Tami Graves persona. She joined the group at the pond, which included Sarah.

"That was some freaky storm," Tami announced as she joined the group.

Sarah gave her a hug. "Where were you?"

"I was walking home from dinner when the lights went out and the wind started blowing really hard. Looks like the power went out just on this block."

"Yeah," agreed a middle-aged man gripping a leash on which a German Shepherd strained. "I'm across the street, down two houses. The houses that back up to my yard never lost lights."

Sarah jumped in. "There really wasn't a storm. Just very gusty wind and some lightning for a few minutes. Really weird."

"Some kind of a micro-burst, I think." The man with the dog was kneeling, trying to soothe his pet. "It sure got the dogs riled up. Must've been a lot of static electricity in the air."

Sarah said, "Well, the center of it seemed to be right at my pond here, but I don't see any damage. No tree limbs down or anything."

Tami had knelt by the dog and was whispering in his ear. He calmed, nuzzling her. "You're a dog whisperer!" his owner said, laughing.

"I do seem to have a way with animals." Tami rose, petting the dog. "Well, I had a brisk walk home and am ready for bed. Good night, all." Tami turned back toward the Dream Catcher.

"I agree with that." Sarah joined her, as the small group quietly bid one another good night and disbursed.

Inside, Sarah invited Tami for a glass of wine, which she politely refused citing exhaustion. Sarah seemed reluctant to let her go. "I'm worried about the Jordans," she confessed. "They haven't returned."

"Don't you give all the guests a front door key? They'll probably let themselves in." Tami tried to reassure her. Not giving Sarah a chance to continue the conversation Tami added, "Good night," and closed her door behind her, letting out the human sigh of relief that she had come to enjoy.

Once in her room Tami lay on the bed assessing the situation. She had battled and escaped this renegade twice. He obviously had a hold on the Synons who followed him. She still had no inkling of who he was or the total strength of his renegade band. Feeling weakened, she allowed herself to fall into the restorative state of Synon sleep.

＊　＊　＊

Even though the renegades had sufficient control of the computer network that a small contingent could keep the humans at bay while their leader took care of other business, the renegade leader didn't like to be outside for long. He was convinced that this electronic environment was his destiny. And he its. He hurried back to his new domain, confident that he would prevail.

＊　＊　＊

In the Realm, the strongest Synons had formed a network to monitor TuMa'Aye Gra'Vay on Earth. They met with Tork, who concurred that she maintained a keen link with Earth's natural life as well as The Living World for protection. They were unable to discern the identity of the renegade Synon leader who had dared to attack the queen and absorb the essences of two Synons. He was an abomination. Having never experienced anything at all similar they were at a loss as to how to proceed. Their only recourse was to turn to The Living World for guidance.

＊　＊　＊

"Good morning." Tami heard Sarah Hawke knock loudly on a door. "Mr. Jordan? Mrs. Jordan?"

Tami stopped the call she was about to dial and walked out into the hallway. Sarah stood before the Jordans' closed door. "Is something wrong, Sarah?"

"I don't think the Jordans came home last night. They're early risers but haven't appeared this morning." Concerned, Sarah went to the office and called their room phone. It could be heard ringing with no answer. She got the key and reluctantly put it in the door. "They always kept their door locked when they were in the room," she said. Sarah opened the door slowly, again calling their names. The drapes were closed, and the bed was made.

Tami entered the room, switching on a light and opening the drapes. She went into the bathroom. Sarah followed. It was clean, neat, and dry. Toothbrushes stood neatly in glasses. Two travel kits sat zippered on the counter. They checked the closet and found clothes hanging above two suitcases.

Tami opened dresser drawers to find neatly folded pajamas. "It does look like they were never here last night," Tami mused. The distinct residue of Synon energy faintly permeated the room. She had suspected the Jordans but was unable to catch any Synon signature from them at the only time she had been in their presence a couple of nights before. They must have developed a strong barrier.

"I should call Jeff." Sarah started toward the room phone.

"Wait." Tami caught her arm. "The police might want to process the room. Don't contaminate anything else. We've probably already touched too much." She recalled flashes from the various TV police procedural dramas she'd absorbed in the Internet.

Sarah looked stricken. "Do you think they've been harmed?"

"The police usually don't follow up missing persons reports until twenty-four hours have passed. Maybe we should wait until tonight. Besides, the police are dealing with a crisis right now."

Sarah looked at her, perplexed. "They are? How do you know? There was nothing in the morning news. Oh, there was a report of some kind of computer glitch. It didn't sound too important, though."

Cover story, Tami thought. Standard. She tried to smooth over her too quick exclamation about a crisis. "You're probably right. I think the channel I watched sensationalized it for effect."

"Nevertheless, I'm going to call Jeff for advice." Sarah was already marching into the office.

Tami sighed, enjoying this human indulgence. Now what? she thought. I'll bet they find no fingerprints or DNA in that room for anyone other than Sarah and the staff. Sarah will say I was also there. They'll wonder why I left no fingerprints. I need to go back and wipe down the space. She heard Sarah's voice. The room had been left open. Did she have time to clean it before Sarah hung up and possibly found her? She could work fast. She went into the storeroom and found disinfectant cleaning wipes. Hoping they would do the trick, she covered every surface she could recall that she or Sarah had touched. It might seem odd that absolutely no fingerprints were found, which could lead the cops to conclude that it had been cleaned, but they would get no confession from her, Sarah, or the maid. The fading Synon energy trace was still identifiable.

She heard Sarah's voice, loud and insistent. Then the phone hit its cradle with a loud noise. Tami ran into her own room, stashed the box of wipes, then went back toward the office. Sarah came out of the office looking angry. "Do you believe they wouldn't even answer the phone? It just rang and rang. The police headquarters! Jeff's cell sent me right to voicemail. I was livid! All I could do was yell at their answering machines!"

"Well, they are having computer problems. Maybe it's affecting the voicemail that usually answers and routes calls."

"This is very disturbing. The Jordans are elderly. They're strangers here. Maybe I should try 911."

"No." Tami's tone was adamant. "They'll be busy enough with real emergencies. We don't know what happened. Maybe the Jordans are," she thought a moment, "con artists. They wanted to skip out on their bill."

"And leave all their belongings behind?"

"Maybe they had to get out of town quickly. They could be criminals on the lam, or spies, or—"

As she strode into the kitchen Sarah quipped, "Tami, you must watch way too much TV! I'll wait a while and see if Jeff returns my call."

Tami returned to her own room to analyze the shocking truth she had just discovered. The Jordans were Synons. I've lost my edge, she thought. It must be from focusing so intently on appearing human. I wonder how long the Jordans have been here. Have they acquired a human "smell" that masks their true natures? Does that happen to all Synons who stay here any length of time? How is it they were at the same B&B as me? It seems like too much of a coincidence. Unless there are so many Synons here that I could run into them anywhere. And I haven't. Am I being tracked and watched? She dialed Jeff's cell and left an urgent message for him to call her saying it had to do with their dinner conversation, which could be all too real.

Just as Tami ended the call a horrible thought struck her. I'm at this B&B because of Jeff. He sent me here. Did he already know what I was and that the Jordans were here? Were they in cahoots? No, that's crazy. I found Jeff first by accident. I did wonder that it was so quick after my arrival on Earth. Is there some elaborate plot to control me? She sighed again, beginning to really like this human expression of frustration. And, of course, Sarah could be right, she admitted to herself. I've rapidly ingested extreme numbers of TV shows, movies, mystery and science fiction novels and other forms of the fictionalized stories humans love so much. I've developed a vivid humanized imagination and their penchant for conspiracy theories.

She turned on her TV hoping it might distract her. A story was unfolding about a strange micro-burst of wind that had hit a section of the city arboretum, apparently the night before. The correspondent was interviewing a meteorologist who insisted that the winds had been calm and no such event had been recorded, although he acknowledged that the region had recently seen more storms and unusual weather phenomena than was the average. The camera panned showing trees uprooted and tangled, even large clots of sod upturned.

The ringing phone averted her attention and Tami was surprised to hear Jeff's voice. "What's going on there?"

"You haven't spoken to Sarah yet?"

"I needed a laugh. I called you first." His voice held no mirth.

She ignored the sarcasm, pushing aside the human hurt that tried to sidetrack her. "This couple, the Jordans, who disappeared, were Sy—" she caught herself, "simply odd. They never used the room that their belongings have occupied for two days and nights. I just have a weird feeling about them."

"What do you want from me? You know this network incursion has to be my only focus. They haven't been gone long enough to be classified as missing persons, and that call has to go to your precinct, not me."

Why had she called him? She should have concocted a story first. "I think they might be connected to the invading cyber entities." That's all she could think of.

"Okay, I'll bite. Why?" He sounded incredulous.

"I saw the Jordans kind of shimmer, like they were fading and about to wink out. Literally, I mean like they were disappearing before my eyes. Then they made a hasty excuse to leave. Remember when we discussed shape-shifters? If your cyber invaders are like that, it could work to your advantage. They might only be able to hold a shape for a certain amount of time." It was a perfect opportunity to plant this notion in Jeff's mind.

"Just because you think you saw these people shimmer, you conclude that they're shape- shifters? And that they're connected to our cyber intruders? Tami, I'm beginning to wonder how you got a journalism assignment dealing with science."

"Oh, no," Tami interjected quickly, taking a new tack. "I was really tired, and it was probably just the wine affecting me that made them appear to shimmer. It just took my thought processes to our discussion and then this idea just popped into my head that your intruders could be shape-shifters who…"

"I'm just too busy to listen to this nutty stuff. I gotta go." He clicked off.

Tami stood holding her phone, emotions overwhelming her; she knew how humans felt when they needed to cry. She mentally shook herself, metaphorically shaking off the unwanted feelings that were affecting her thought patterns. They were disruptive, interesting only from an observational viewpoint. More and more she was seeing how humans made decisions within a constant emotional vortex, and she resented the personal intrusion.

She told Sarah that Jeff had instructed them to call the local precinct and Sarah immediately did so. When she finally got someone to take her call she was told an officer would be there that evening and in the meantime not to touch the room.

All right, Tami thought petulantly. Let them investigate. We'll see what comes of it. Jeff Hawke might be surprised.

The sense of connection between her and Jeff had diminished almost as if he had deliberately severed it. She understood how he could scoff at her suggestions, but his behavior was confusing. She had to focus on her duty. After all, she was Queen of the Realm— even if Jeff Hawke would never believe her if she told him. Concentrating on her true nature and responsibility would rid her of these unwanted and unsettling human feelings he engendered. Beyond what she recognized as a personal and risky attachment to Jeff, he was a link to the Synon attack. She had been able to get into the Internet through the library's servers and should be able to do it again. She stared at her closed laptop wondering if she could essentially hack into the city network through the Dream Catcher's wi-fi. She opened the laptop then abruptly closed it. She was not prepared for a confrontation with the cyber Synons, especially alone. She had felt Tork's presence in the recesses of her mind and was certain he was aware of what she was experiencing. Maybe she should search for a Passageway and return to the Realm to formulate a plan for her fellow Synons to confront the renegades as a unified force. She could not deny what the consequences would be: the unthinkable —a war between Synons.

*　　*　　*

That evening an officer and a crime scene technician came to the Dream Catcher.

The officer questioned and took statements from both Sarah and Tami. While he did so the technician processed the Jordans' room. While Tami maintained her Synon calm the questioning rattled Sarah, who burst into tears. "Why are you acting like we're guilty? We just want to know where the Jordans are and if they're all right," she sobbed.

"If they've disappeared, you were the last people to see them that we know of," he replied, unruffled by her tears. "That makes you persons of interest."

At that moment, the technician motioned for the officer to speak privately with her. Tami tried to reassure Sarah. "This is routine," she said.

The officer returned wearing a grim expression. "Someone has thoroughly cleaned the room in question. No fingerprints or DNA traces were found. Did you clean the room today, Miss Hawke?" He glared at Sarah.

"No. Tami mentioned that we shouldn't." She sat quietly sobbing.

He turned his attention to Tami. "Miss Graves, why did you suggest that the room not be cleaned?"

"I watch a lot of crime shows on TV," she replied in a matter-of-fact tone. "They find evidence that solves the crimes. I didn't want us to taint anything."

"Didn't the two of you go into the room this morning?"

Sarah started to speak, but Tami replied quickly, throwing a warning glance at Sarah. "I don't know that we touched anything. We mostly looked around. We could see their suitcases and some clothes through the open closet door. There was also stuff in the bathroom. The bed appeared not to have been used." She was glad that she had decided not to clean the doorknob and door since Sarah had obviously opened it. Tami thought she had lied as adeptly as any human.

The officer peered intently at her. "The only fingerprints found were Miss Hawkes' on the door. No other fingerprints or DNA were found anywhere in the room. Can you explain that, Miss Hawkes?"

As she answered the officer, Sarah was looking at Tami curiously. "The Jordans checked in two days ago and appeared to be sleeping in that room. I can't explain what you found. We do clean daily, but she said she was allergic to many cleaning products so they requested that we not clean their room. Perhaps they were cleaning it themselves." Tami was not surprised to learn this.

The officer sat quietly watching both women for a moment. "I'll need to take the register they signed. We'll do a background check on them. There's no evidence that any harm has come to them. No bodies matching their descriptions have been found. It looks like they might have disappeared on purpose; our background check will tell us more. Without further evidence this is not the kind of case we can expend a lot of resources on. We'll see what we can find quickly. We'll have to ask that you leave the room untouched and that both of you not leave town until this is resolved."

Sarah was upset; Tami's mind was whirling. She was thinking that these "Jordans" knew who, or at least what, she was and decided to get out of the Dream Catcher. Why they didn't just check out was still a mystery. Maybe they made the decision while they were out and just decided not to risk returning. They might have even conferred with other Synons.

It made her think about how tenuous life was for Synons pretending to be human. TuMa'Aye Gra'Vay had found it fairly easy to fabricate the basic elements of a human body, but fingerprints eluded her, and she was certain that applied to other Synons. If they were arrested their only choice would be to return to their energy form and escape, abandoning their personas. If they had built lives and relationships that would all be lost. And to what extent were they able to form relationships with people? In the past, Synons never got close to humans. She wondered just how long the Jordans had managed to pull off their subterfuge. They wore the appearance of older people. Had they been here so long that they had aged their personas? She needed to contact other Synons. She needed to learn about how and why they lived here as people.

The police had barred the door to the Jordans' room with yellow "crime scene" tape reminding them of the troubling mystery. Sarah was distraught. "I should call a locksmith to change the front door lock. Their key could have been stolen."

"It's pretty late now," Tami reminded her. "You do have the inside bolt that you use when everyone is safely in for the night. That should be sufficient until you can have the lock changed tomorrow."

Sarah agreed, then checked the rest of the locks twice and left extra lights on when they retired to their separate rooms for the night.

■   ■   ■

The next day Tami began thinking about how to reach other Synons. She could mentally connect with the Realm to ask if the whereabouts were known of any who had specific missions nearby. That would require a lot of energy and a secluded natural setting. She went online to research nearby nature preserves and parks outside of cities. Such a place might harbor a Passageway, but she knew she couldn't travel right away.

She suddenly felt the urgent need to get out. She walked a while and found herself in the park where Cat and the other animals had helped her. It was strange to now walk through it as just one of many human strollers. There was no hint of Synons and only the faint connection to The Living World generated by the greenery, lake, and wildlife. Had it only been a few days ago that she quivered in the form of a small creature communicating only with others of the animal world? It felt like centuries had passed. She had experienced and learned so much. More significantly, she was more human than she had ever been. She now had a fundamental comprehension of the complexity of their minds and emotions, and that led to her understanding how and why Synons had chosen to live here posing as humans. She wondered if others beyond the renegades had ventured into the Internet or found other ways to quickly absorb knowledge that helped them maintain human personas. Perhaps they had gradually gathered information with the passing of time and human interaction.

Tami wanted to see Cat again and found the spot where she had met him. She sent out a mental message. Knowing he was wary of humans she toyed with the idea of changing to a cat herself. It might be refreshing. If impractical. Even though there were no other people in her immediate vicinity they were too close, and in daylight it was too risky to try crawling into the bushes to change form. The cats probably hid during the day to sleep and came out at night to hunt for food. How could she locate them? She walked slowly along a maze-like path through the hedge then felt a warmth along her leg—Cat.

She impulsively picked him up and cuddled him. He didn't struggle, gazing up at her with vivid green eyes. "You came back to see me." The impression sounded like joyful words in her "mind's ear."

"I'll never forget you." she sent love to him, as an idea formed. "I came here to see if you were all right and for another purpose." She went to a bench and sat down. Cat sat in her lap, still looking at her. "Are you aware of any Passageways nearby? Gateways between your world and mine. They wouldn't be visible, but they radiate a connection with The Living World. Synons from my world use them to travel to this one."

"No. I've never noticed anything like that. Are you going to be a human now?"

"No. This is temporary. I must eventually return to the Realm." She paused, an idea flashing in her mind. "Would you like to live with a human who loves animals? Could you adjust to living in a house and being a pet?"

"I did that once. When I was a kitten. It was nice until they started yelling at me, then kicking and hitting me. The children cried and the adults brought me to this park and left me. At least they didn't kill me."

"I might know someone who would love you and never abandon you. He is gone a lot, so you would be alone in his house, but would be comfortable and cared for."

"Is he like you? Can he talk to me?"

"I don't think so. The two of you would bond, though. He's very busy right now with a big project. I'll bring him to meet you soon. In the meantime, please be on the lookout for possible Passageways or others like me. I'm sorry that I have to go now." She leaned down and kissed his head. His fur was surprising soft for a feral. "I'll see you soon." Despite the chill between Tami and Jeff she knew instinctively that Jeff and Cat would bond. She had no qualms about uniting them.

She returned to the Dream Catcher around noon, having failed to find the slightest trace of a Passageway. She felt alone and trapped.

■　■　■

Jeff Hawke had the ability to tightly focus his mind on a single task, and the task at hand required all of the brain power he possessed.

Despite several days of digging into the guts of the codes that built the city's computer software, the team had made no real progress in eradicating the intruders. Codes were being dismantled at an alarming rate, replaced by new indecipherable script. They had no way of knowing the intruders' intentions. It was surreal. Jeff felt like he was immersed in the video game challenge of his life, and like many games, the stakes in this one were extremely high. To Jeff it resembled all too eerily the prevalent game theme of a life and death struggle between good and evil.

Sudden waves of regret and melancholy rolled through him. His analytic mind recognized that he was demonstrating the clichéd psychology term "defense mechanism" by deliberately pushing Tami Graves away because he was fearful of his growing attraction to her. He wanted to take back the harsh words he had so coldly uttered to her, yet he had no clue as to how to go about it. Then he remembered a promise he'd made.

CHAPTER SEVEN

As Tami entered the Dream Catcher Sarah caught her. "We've got a fun invitation for tonight I'm anxious to tell you about. You mentioned an interest in my uncle's Nature group."

Tami had been distracted, half listening; now she focused on Sarah. "Yes."

"They're having a potluck dinner and a presentation tonight. It's at the Native American Cultural Center. I could introduce you to people."

"Jeff mentioned an upcoming event. This must be it."

"Yes. He texted to remind me about it and suggested I take you. Of course, he can't come. There's some mess going on at his work."

Tami was even more confused about Jeff's behavior, but she was relieved that he seemed to be making a gesture by taking time to suggest that Sarah take her to this event. "Okay," she quickly responded. "Thanks for inviting me. Can I get something to take?"

"Oh no. My freezer is always crammed with stuff. We can raid it."

Just before they left, Sarah answered a call from the police. When she hung up she turned to Tami with a concerned look. "The Jordans have an apartment in Philadelphia. Local police checked and it was locked up. Neighbors said they seldom saw them, even though they had lived there for years. For now, the police are dropping it. They can't devote any resources to it and will be by tomorrow to remove the tape. Apparently something big is going on that is preoccupying them."

Tami knew what was going on but kept silent.

■   ■   ■

The Native American Cultural Center was an old brick building in what was called a "transitional" neighborhood. Dilapidated and crumbling buildings stood next to those that had been renovated and now housed various businesses on the ground floors with apartments above.

The center's first floor opened onto a large area that was filled with folding metal chairs. On the walls were various types of Native American artifacts and art depicting traditional Native American life. Through an archway Tami saw another room with mismatched sofas and chairs arranged for small group privacy and walls lined with bookcases. In the back of the building people bustled about placing food on the long pass-through that opened from the kitchen onto the dining room, which was furnished with wooden picnic tables and attached benches.

Sarah said, "On the second floor is a small museum you'll want to see. It's an overview of the regional Native Americans. Let's take our food to the kitchen and I'll introduce you to anyone I know." As they walked she continued. "The Living

World Nature Organization uses this facility. It's attracting young people. Tonight's program is by high school students, so I might not know everybody. We'll just get acquainted."

Tami was suddenly a bit apprehensive. She had never really mingled in a large social gathering and feared she'd have to talk about herself. She was soon meeting a variety of people whose warmth and friendliness put her at ease. None asked prying questions, mostly just welcoming her. She saw an interesting mix of genders and people aged from children through the elderly. Most appeared to be Caucasian, although there were a few African Americans sprinkled in and a number of people who looked as if they could be Native American. The spread of food made her think of the stories about the first Thanksgiving Europeans and Indians shared. There was turkey and ham and a wide variety of vegetables and desserts. Tami wished she could actually enjoy eating instead of just transforming what she ingested directly into energy. She took small amounts of several vegetables, remarking to her tablemates that she was a vegetarian. She was surprised that of the five she sat with three others chimed in that they were also. While she was disappointed that no one at their table was Native American, they were all avid about the Living World "movement" as they called it. "We are the most destructive species in the history of the world," a young woman declared.

"More so than dinosaurs?" her preteen son challenged.

Tami spoke up. "I think so. People plunder the Earth's resources to make things for themselves and have scarred a large portion of the world with their artificial cities. No other creature on Earth has done that."

Everyone at the table was looking at her: Sarah, the mother and son, and an older couple. Sarah exclaimed, "I had no idea you were so adamant, Tami. You and Jeff should get along really well. You sound like him."

"That's a good thing to know." Tami grinned.

A tall, wiry man who looked ancient stood and the room went silent. He had long white hair tied at the back with leather. "Friends, once again we give thanks to be sharing food and friendship. Let's take a few minutes to clean up and put any leftovers in our refrigerator. Tomorrow we'll invite the homeless in for lunch." He mesmerized Tami. She tried to penetrate his mind but found it tightly closed. In a deep voice he continued. "Then let's move to the general area. Two of our young members have created presentations for us."

They all migrated to the metal folding chairs in the large room. Tami noticed that a screen had been lowered and a projector sat on a table, cables linking it to two laptop computers at which sat a teen-aged boy and girl. The girl stood and spoke. Her voice was surprisingly clear and commanding for her age. "Hello everyone. Thank you so much for coming. First we want to thank Mr. Jeff Hawke for this projector. It allows us to show you our videos directly from the computers to the screen." Tami and Sarah smiled at each other. This generosity was another glimpse into Jeff's complex character and to his dedication to this "movement."

The young girl continued. "I am Misty Donahue, and my presentation is about the Cherokee alphabet. Could someone get the lights?" As the lights dimmed the video began with magnificent scenery within the lands of the Eastern Band of the Cherokee in Western North Carolina: high, gushing waterfalls and vistas resembling a sea of mountains. Misty Donahue's voice narrated. "The Cherokees developed the first written Native American language. It was created by a man called Sequoyah in the early1800s. His English name was George Gist." As she spoke, an image appeared showing a lifelike painting of a distinguished-looking man wearing a rounded headdress of deep crimson. He had a long pipe in his mouth and held a large piece of paper on which appeared symbols that looked similar to hieroglyphs.

The voice-over narration continued. "Sequoyah created what is known as a syllabary. Each written character represents a syllable. He taught others to use it, and by 1828 the first Native American newspaper, called the *Cherokee Phoenix*, was published in New Echota, Georgia, built on the model of traditional American towns and designated by the Cherokee as their capital. Tragically, it was here that the Trail of Tears was instigated when the eastern Cherokee were dragged from their homes and forced to relinquish their lands east of the Mississippi and physically removed by the United States to Oklahoma. About four thousand of fifteen thousand died on this forced march. In his presentation Jeremy will tell you more about this and how the Eastern Band has thrived. I'd like to show you a close-up image of Sequoyah's Syl—"

Everything went dark. The quiet hum of the refrigerator ceased, then restarted as dim lights appeared along the baseboards and doors, indicating that generators had kicked in. The tall man's voice resonated over the low murmur that arose. "The generators should keep the refrigerator running along with the few emergency lights. Alana just stepped outside to see how far the outage seems to be. We should be used to this," he said

chuckling, "from the spate of recent storms we've endured."
There were nervous giggles from the group.

The young woman, Alana's, voice rang out from the front of
the room. "No lights anywhere. Street and traffic lights are out.
No buildings are lit."

The older man now held a mobile phone, which cast a faint
bluish light onto his craggy face. "I just got a text from Jeff
Hawke, who works with the police department. He says this is a
city-wide outage that could last a long time and advises we stay
put." The crowd's murmur was now tinged with apprehension.
"If any of you have reasons that you must leave, go ahead; please
be extra careful driving. All of you are welcome to stay as long as
you need to. As you know we also function as a homeless shelter
when there is severe weather. We have a pantry full of provi-
sions, including blankets and pillows." The murmur became
a cacophony of voices as people discussed the situation. Many
hurriedly left.

"I think we should stay," Sarah said breathlessly to Tami.
"I don't want to drive back to the inn. I have no other guests.
I'd rather just stay here, especially since Jeff suggested it. Is that
okay with you?"

Tami nodded. "I agree." Her mind was whirling. Jeff had
taken the time to text the Center, indicating that the situation
might be dangerous. Anything could be happening with the
intruders. They could be initiating a full-scale cyberattack on the
region's power infrastructure and possibly beyond. She hated not
being in the center of the situation where she could possibly take
some action. Ironically, she had wanted to learn about the Living
World group and the Native American Cultural Center, and here
she was trapped with them. She might as well make the best of it.

"Who is the man that seems to be in charge?" she asked Sarah.

"Lewis Henderson. He's one of the founders of the Living World movement. And he is the administrator of this center."

"Is he Native American?"

"Oh, yes. Let's go meet him. I want to ask what I can do anyway." She led Tami along the perimeter of the room to where Lewis Henderson towered above a small knot of people near the kitchen. As they approached, even in the shadowed room, he recognized her and broke out into a grin. "Sarah. I'm glad you're here." His dark, penetrating eyes bore into Tami's.

Sarah turned to Tami. "I'd like you to meet Tami Graves. Jeff sent her to the Dream Catcher." Henderson thrust out a large hand. "So you're also friends with Jeff." He said it as a statement rather than a question.

She grasped the hand and once again reached for his mind. It was serene but closed to her. "I'm glad to meet you." She returned his penetrating gaze. "Jeff and I are more acquaintances than friends. We met by chance. Quite coincidentally, I was told about the Living World organization here and learned that Jeff's uncle had given it that name. I'm interested in the concept."

Unhampered by the dark, she glimpsed a twinkle in Henderson's eye. "I'm sure you are." An enigmatic smile appeared on the rugged face.

Sarah interrupted. "I feel uncomfortable just standing here when others are working. What can I do?"

Henderson seemed to have forgotten her. "You can help in the pantry getting out blankets and pillows." He gestured behind the kitchen.

"Okay." She looked at Tami. "Want to help, Tami?"

The question jerked Tami out of the deep place she had gone. "Oh, sure."

"I have another task for Ms. Graves," Henderson said.

Sarah looked a bit flustered. "Oh, okay. See you later, Tami." She gave the two of them another perplexed look and walked away.

The enigmatic smile widened a bit. "It's still early. People aren't ready to go to sleep; they're too keyed up. As you can see, a group is huddling over there with a battery radio. Others might like a quieter pastime, like yourself, I suspect."

"I was hoping to peruse your library," Tami admitted.

Henderson caught Alana's attention and motioned her over. "Alana, this is Tami. She can help you with the battery-powered lamps. Then I think she wants to use one of them in the library."

"Sure. Glad to meet you, Tami." Alana grinned. She had strikingly beautiful bone structure and long black hair. Tami noticed that she wore a beaded ring similar to Jeff's. A strange feeling gripped her. Perhaps Jeff and this lovely Native American woman were... "Come on. I'll lead you to our storage room." Alana's voice pulled Tami back to the moment. She mentally brushed away the whiff of jealousy.

When they reached the storage room, Alana noticed Tami's obvious amazement at the amount of supplies. "We try to be prepared to help the community in any kind of emergency," she said as she pulled a large container off a shelf and opened it. "Here are lamps and batteries. I'll set up a couple so we can see better and show you how to install the batteries. We leave them out to preserve them."

They soon had an array of lamps standing inside the container that Alana easily hefted. "We'll distribute them around the first floor. We're discouraging people from going to other floors. There's plenty of room down here anyway."

There were small groups of people everywhere, some quietly talking, a couple with radios, and many trying unsuccessfully to find data on their cell phones since the networks were jammed with too many users at once. They were all grateful for the lamps offered them.

Soon there were only a couple of lamps left. "You've been a big help, Tami. I think you've earned a break. Take this lamp and get comfortable in the common room. Feel free to browse the library." Alana handed her the lamp with a wide grin.

"I think I'll take you up on that offer." Tami smiled. "Maybe you can help me. I'd like to do some research on legends and mythology. You can just lead me to the right section. I love to browse in books."

"Okay. Let's get you as close as we can to the kind of book you need."

Tami was enthralled with the titles and took a stack of books to a chair where she began rapidly turning pages and assimilating information. As other people drifted in and sat nearby she forced herself to slow down to the pace of a human scanning tables of contents, indexes, and pages.

She knew that all First Peoples of the Earth had rich cultural traditions, conveyed through the generations by visual imagery and storytelling. There was a common thread of connection to The Living World. A pervasive strand was the acceptance of spiritual beings as part of the everyday natural world.

There were tales of human encounters with such spirits. Tami smiled. Acutely aware that such people regarded The Living World as part of themselves, she was certain that some of the spirits spoken of were Synons. She sighed wistfully. Things were so different now.

"Have you found what you were looking for?" Lewis Henderson's voice drifted from the darkness as Tami sat engrossed.

"Not the exact thing I was searching for, but I found other related material that might help me, uh, in my research project. I'm a journalist, you know."

"Of course." His face crinkled into a grin. "Take whatever books you want with you. I trust you to return them."

"I don't need them—" She caught herself. Although the books' contents were catalogued in her mind, a human would need the books to refer to. "Thank you. That's so generous of you. I have a couple here that I'd like to borrow." She picked out two of the volumes and set them aside.

She realized that her lamp was the only one still lit. In the darkness she saw people curled up on the sofas and a few in the comfy chairs asleep. She didn't need illumination to see that cots were set up in the common room and more people slept wrapped in blankets on the floor.

"I seem to be the only one still awake." She laughed.

"Except for me," Henderson noted. "I'm about to turn in myself. I brought you a blanket and pillow." He handed the items to her. "I'm afraid all the cots and sofas are taken. Can you sleep in this chair?"

She was beginning to long for solitude and Synon respite, although grateful for the chance to rest her mind while maintaining the Tami persona. "I think I've probably been dozing a bit anyway," she said. "I'll be fine here. Thank you."

"Good night." He said and left.

She hadn't found exactly what she hoped to in the books, but she had found something that sparked an idea. Time to let it gestate. She wrapped her sham body in the blanket and lay her head on the pillow, clearing her mind and letting it drift. She felt more at peace than at any time since arriving on this tumultuous planet.

■　■　■

The Cyber Terror Geeks, as Jeff's group had been dubbed, rationed precious generator power to specific spots within the vast computer network linking the municipal infrastructure.

Electrical power was provided to the city by a private company, and several of its key IT members, as well as representatives from the local Homeland Security office, had joined them in the city's "bunker," a state-of-the-art Emergency Operations Center. It had been established after the "9-11" World Trade Center attacks and used several times when rogue hurricanes brought flooding to their city. The considerable brain power, expertise, and experience of the team proved as ineffective against this enemy as snowballs shot from a cannon. They were stumped. Compounding their astonishment were signs of intense bursts of energy throughout the system that could not be from the feeble generator power they were spoon-feeding to carefully chosen points.

Jeff's precision focus wavered, and phantom thoughts flitted into his mind as Tami's outrageous ideas lingered, haunting.

Could this really be some kind of alien invasion? Could these really be intelligent entities within the network rather than hackers working at computers outside it, as everyone assumed? He had decided not yet to make any mention of such notions to his teammates or superiors. A new thought exploded: maybe they had similar suspicions but were purposefully not expressing them. Who knew what Homeland was aware of or preparing for? He mentally chuckled. Tami should work for a "what if" think tank. His mood turned grim as thoughts he had tried to bury tunneled to the surface. How was it that Tami suddenly appeared just before this attack? Did she have some involvement with it? Maybe her cockeyed suggestions were simply red herrings designed to draw his attention away from the true nature of the incursion.

"We're totally locked out of our entire grid," one of the power company techs growled. "It's anyone's guess now when we'll ever get power back. If ever."

"This might be terrorism. The entire region, especially the State Capitol area, is now in high emergency alert mode. I'm recommending to the mayor that a curfew be implemented where there is no power," a grim-faced Homeland Security officer injected. The middle-aged woman rose from her chair and started toward the door. "If this continues martial law could be enacted. We'll need full-scale disaster and security mobilization. Better talk to the brass."

■　　■　　■

Tami felt rejuvenated after about an hour of "sleep" in the chair.

She reached out and felt a palpable connection to The Living World. Her questions at dinner had yielded information about the various areas of the center. She let her mind drift through the multistory building, starting at the top floor where she had learned that rare and precious artifacts were stored, some very ancient, but she felt no unusual power. She worked her way down the floors of the building and was astonished to find a strong concentration of what seemed like Synon energy in the basement. Why hadn't she sensed this before? Lewis Henderson radiated an obvious connection; despite his closed mind, she had sensed no Synon essence. There appeared to be other Synons here. She sensed no hostile spirit, only peaceful, open Synon minds at rest.

Her humanized body was reacting to the shock with rapid breath and pulse. She felt the irises of her eyes widen. Then elation flooded her. Here was a group of Synons. She could enlist their help instead of spending precious time searching for others. They would understand everything. She quietly made her way to the basement room where she sensed the group. It was dark, but she didn't need eyes to find those she sought. She touched each mind in turn, bringing them into synchronicity. They began to stir and one by one rose and joined her, wearing their human forms. She beckoned them to a small storage room. Although it wasn't needed, by habit one had brought a flashlight that he switched on. It cast a halo glow. He placed it on a shelf where the light spilled across the small room and faces came into view. Tami saw about ten people, men and women of all ages. She was not surprised to find Lewis Henderson among them, his smile no longer enigmatic, was now broad, his eyes crinkled. "So you found us," he said.

"I'd like to know how you block so completely," she blurted.

"It's taken millennia for Synons living here to develop and pass along the technique of impenetrable shielding," he replied. "And, of course, we'll share it; more important issues face us now, as you so well know. However, we would like to take this moment to welcome the Queen of the Realm."

"Thank you." Tami's response was almost impatient. Her mind was racing. "At the Dream Catcher there were two Synons right under my nose," Tami muttered, "so well blocked that even I couldn't identify them."

"The Jordan couple," Lewis nodded, sadness in his expression. "They had been here for centuries and only wanted to be left alone, then the renegades destroyed them."

"The Arboretum?" Tami recalled the news story about a freak wind storm the night the renegades attacked her, causing a small, localized weather phenomenon, the same night the Jordans disappeared.

Lewis nodded. "There was no trace of them when we went that night to investigate. The renegades simply sucked up their energy and absorbed it."

Trying to push down the revulsion such news churned up, Tami told them about the attack on her the same night and the cyberspace encounters with the renegades. "They are the cause of this blackout. If they get beyond the city computer network who knows what will happen."

Alana looked impatient. "They've taken humanity's innovation and turned it against them. I think they want domination. We need to stop them."

Lewis Henderson touched her shoulder. "I fear you're right, of course, Alana, but we need to carefully plan how to do that. I'm concerned about their timing. Earth is in distress from rapid ecosystem destruction and climate change accelerated by human disregard. These renegades are taking advantage of this turmoil. We need to find a way to neutralize them without barging into this human computer network after them. We are novices and they are experienced. The last thing we want is the one thing that has never happened: a war between Synons."

Tami spoke. "We don't know how long they've been exploring and learning about this Internet. It connects the entire world. I have to agree with Alana." She nodded toward the young woman. "The renegades want to control Earth. They have abandoned their mission to protect The Living World, going so far as to verbally ridicule it." Her tone and demeanor changed as she asked, "How long have you known I was here?"

"From the moment you arrived. You broadcast widely." Lewis laughed. "We knew the renegades were initiating a plan but couldn't pinpoint it. We thought if we left you alone you might find them. Or they would find you. And we were right." His serious countenance didn't offer a hint of pleasure at his revelation.

"So you used me as bait?" A raised eyebrow and slight crook of the mouth replaced the sting of her reply with humor that quickly vanished. "Was Jeff Hawke in on it?"

"No," Lewis answered. "He's not a Synon. Jeff's always had a strong connection to The Living World, despite being a technology genius."

"Because he is Native American?"

"No. We've found others like him all over this nation and globally, from very different ethnic and cultural backgrounds."

"Jeff and these others appear to have somehow retained the connection of their ancestors while it has faded in most." Her tone turned urgent. "I gather there are more Synons here?"

"Many, around this world," Lewis answered. "There is no unity, however. They fear discovery and cling together in small hidden cells. They take different paths, most feeling that they can best achieve their purpose to protect The Living World by influencing human attitudes and actions from within their own societies."

"We must prioritize cultivating these people like Jeff. First, we have to deal with the crisis at hand."

Tami noticed heads nodding and many eyes averted. "Are we united here and ready to confront the renegades?" Eyes widened and bodies became a little more erect in unconscious response to her suddenly regal and commanding demeanor.

A younger woman scowled. "We need to know what we face."

"All right. I have a plan. But you won't like it."

CHAPTER EIGHT

A glorious swath of pale pink, blue, and yellow painted the sky like swirls of watercolor spilled over the horizon. Weary, raw-nerved citizens greeted the sunrise with skeptical joy. It had been a long night. With no electricity and cell lines jammed and inaccessible people were isolated in small groups or alone. Fortunately, it was early summer and had been comfortable, but a heat wave had been predicted, and if the outage continued, people accustomed to air-conditioning and fans would grow even more frustrated and angry. At dawn they began to venture out, comforted by encountering others. No one had any accurate information about the blackout. Rumors traveled like electricity along the now barren lines. The most prevalent rumor was that martial law was about to be imposed, which would be unprecedented after such a short power outage.

Some store managers tried to open and transact business as best they could without the electronic cash registers and credit card devices they had come to rely upon. At first, people offered what cash they could for supplies, then realized that they might not be able to get more from the banks that were all securely locked down with nonfunctional ATMs. Others took advantage of the situation and looted what they could get regardless of its immediate use. Many shrugged, smirked, and dismissed it as a lost day of productivity. Glitches happen. Take a day off. Not to worry. They'll get it fixed.

Radio and television stations were broadcasting for those who had battery-operated devices or the rare cellular service. With the city government offering only: "We are working on a technical issue," broadcasters scampered to bring in local "experts" to discuss possible causes of the blackout. These included die-hard "I told you so!" doomsday and survivalist types who fueled the rumor mill with the raw materials of discontent and panic.

By mid-morning, city officials spoke at a hastily arranged press briefing in front of city hall trying to reassure the populace that they were not under attack, there had been no nuclear accident, and it was simply an unforeseen technical malfunction that had caused an unfortunate domino effect on the power grid. They had the best people working on it. They urged people to be calm and considerate of one another. This was a time to come together. Check on those who might need help and render it. Conserve supplies and share. Law enforcement was out in force and looters would be arrested. If you had to drive, you should treat all intersections as four way stops. Be courteous. Show the true character of this city.

■　　■　　■

In the "bunker" it didn't matter if it was day or night outside; its self-contained, generator-powered, windowless environment never changed.

Jeff Hawke slouched in his chair, staring at the screen that had been the sole object of his attention for hours. Mysterious code swiftly scrolled like a gushing waterfall. It blurred as his eyelids dropped. "Hawke! Your turn. Take an hour. You're no good to us with your eyes closed." The duty officer nearly barked at him.

Jeff was beyond protesting. He dragged his rangy body out of the chair and hobbled to the door, legs and feet numb from immobility. They were supposed to get up, stretch and walk around every hour, but that protocol had flown by the wayside in this unprecedented emergency.

Craving daylight, Jeff walked outside and down to a small lake surrounded by trees heavy with fresh summer greenery and blossoming flowers. It was empty and quiet. He tried to relax, strolling around the lake. His mind began to calm and clear. A few ducks waddled from the shore into the water, their sharp quacks breaking the silence. He chuckled, watching them dip headfirst into the water, searching for food. There was a pleasant breeze, and blue sky peeked through fluffy clouds. The serenity of Nature was soothing like a balm.

A slight sound behind a weeping willow caused him to turn around. A glow emanated from behind the thick willow limbs that reached for the ground. Then an apparition appeared, and he knew he had gone way too long without sleep. Slowly gliding toward him was a luminous creature. Strands of multicolored light streamed from an exquisite female face, vaguely familiar. The visage alternately morphed into that of a doe, its eyes mirrors of the woman's. Lustrous hair framed the face, flying strands glittering like jewels—golden, raven, chestnut, ebony in color. She wore a flowing white dress and cloak of a material resembling soft leather elaborately embroidered with colorful beads. Her step was silent in the grass as she glided inexorably closer to him.

Jeff stood transfixed. Part of him assumed he was dreaming, yet he had never felt more alert and aware. He stood and waited.

The specter stopped a few feet in front of him. It became fully female, locking eyes with him. She took a step toward him. Abruptly the phantom transformed into a female deer. It stood on four delicate legs, eyes never leaving his. The creature continued its dance of alternating female and deer figures, holding his gaze hostage. At times she appeared solid, then amorphous, translucent. He lost sense of time.

The woman gained substance, standing close to him.

Abruptly he found his voice. "You have captivated me." He felt like a puppet. He would never say something like that.

"That is what I often do." The voice was surprisingly sultry and seductive. "You do know who I am, don't you?" He flung his shock of dark hair in a vigorous head shake.

"As a boy you were fascinated by stories of legendary and mythological beings."

"They populated a lot of video games and movies."

"You also read a lot and heard stories at powwows and gatherings."

How did she know that? He shivered. "All kids love to hear stories about strange creatures," he retorted.

"You recall the stories? Then, in college you did a research paper on archetypical characters that persist across cultures. Like shape-shifters."

"Like you?"

"Yes. I am often called the Deer Woman."

"Okay. Yeah." Jeff muttered as if talking to himself. "I've heard that one." His skeptical nature was beginning to punch through his stupor. "And you're here because?"

"Do you believe that shape-shifters really exist?" She shifted rhythmically between the female and the doe faces.

"Naw, of course not. I guess I'm dreaming."

"Wake up!" she commanded.

"Not working," he slurred. "I'm so tired. Just gotta sit down." He sank to the damp, pungent grass.

She stood over him, now fully in the female form, eyes riveted to his. "You are not asleep." Her voice was sharp, all sultry seduction gone. "This is reality. Stand up!"

Like a marionette whose strings had been yanked, he bolted upright, now standing face to face with her. The face began to morph, like a camera lens changing focus. It blurred then suddenly the face of Tami Graves was before him.

"I should have known!" He backed away. "You do yourself up like a Hollywood Indian maiden and use smoke and mirrors to trick me. I don't know what your game is, but it's really offensive."

"I found this figure in books. You just acknowledged that Deer Woman is found in several cultures. I just wanted to use a familiar archetype to get your attention. My primary goal was to demonstrate that shape-shifters are real."

"If I wasn't an Indian would you have tried that?" he snarled.

"Your research found shape-shifters in cultures all over the world. I'm sorry if choosing an image with some Native American elements was offensive. The paramount issue here is for you to accept that I am a shape-shifter. No stories exist about my true nature. It's alien to you. Revealing it will be shocking. However, I can do that and introduce you to several others like me." She turned and looked behind the stand of willows lining that part of the lake. "It's time," she said.

Lewis Henderson, Alana, and several other people Jeff recognized, stepped from the foliage and stood just behind Tami. Jeff gaped. "You're in on it?" He slapped his head with both hands. "Man, what a wild dream."

Lewis and the others surrounded Jeff in a protective rather than threatening manner. "Jeff. You know that every moment those cyber intruders are growing stronger. We can help you, but you have to believe us." It was Lewis Henderson's voice.

"Okay." Jeff's tone was resigned. "What you got next?" He grinned.

"If that's the only way we can reach you, so be it. Since you're so convinced you're dreaming, I think it's time for us to do the big reveal." Lewis nodded to his colleagues. They all formed a line on either side of Tami Graves. "Synons, show him your true nature," Lewis drawled. As one, the entire group shimmered and glowed, their bodies seeming to disintegrate into thin air, replaced by loose masses of pulsating multicolored light that winked in and out like twinkling stars.

"Good show!" Jeff clapped and grinned. "Now, how the hell can this help with the cyber entities?"

The amorphous masses reformed into the familiar group of people. Tami spoke. "You just called them entities. They are entities. The same as you just saw. A renegade group of the same entities that we are. We just showed you our true form. We are called Synons, and we exist as pure energy-matter, mind, and spirit. We can transform ourselves into most anything by drawing on ambient energy and matter to do it. Humans are aware of the concept of energy and matter as interchangeable."

"Hey, I'm doing some sort of lucid dreaming." His voice now exuded excitement. "My unconscious mind is working on a solution and this is how it's getting me to accept it. Dragging up simplistic Einstein stuff. Okay, Lew, I'm with you. Let's see what the ole brain can conjure. The intruders in our computer network are blobs of energy that can come on out if they want to and turn themselves into the semblance of people. Man, my imagination is about as wild as Tami's to dream this up. No wonder we're drawn to each other. Wait did I say that? Oh, it's okay. This is just a dream. I'm not really admitting anything, and, well, we were kind of becoming friends. Okay." He sank back onto the grass. "So my brain is telling me to consider that these intruders really are some kind of alien or manmade shape-shifting entity that is actually within our software and using our network energy sources for strength, and they're taking over and controlling our entire system—for what purpose?" The group of familiar people who now sat on the grass surrounding him smiled at each other.

Jeff babbled on. "How in hell can I take a notion like this to the brass? I have no proof at all. I need to find out who is behind it. How can I get it? I can't go in the network and interview these things."

"We can go in there." Lewis's deep voice resonated.

Jeff came alert. "Whoa. That was weird. It was almost like a real voice penetrating through my dream fog. "We can go in there." He repeated what he'd heard. He giggled, then whooped. "If the intruders are really these energy beings and there are other entities like them out here who are good—Whoaaa! Super video game! I gotta write this down. Bad entities versus good entities. What do these dream entities call themselves?"

"Synons." The disembodied energy swirls reappeared, with Lewis Henderson's voice emanating from them.

"Synons," Jeff repeated. "Synonymous. Entities that are similar or the same as each other? Blobs that can become just like humans? Is that it?"

"Much more. All living things are synonymous and within The Living World, which is all that is. Humans perceive it in varied ways."

"The Living World!" My uncle's name for our conservation group. That's how my mind came up with it, of course. The old Gaia myth that the Earth is alive."

"It is."

"Okay, voice."

"Synons exist to maintain and nourish the links between those living on Earth and The Living World. You will understand in time. Right now, you need to sleep. Lie back." Jeff needed no coaxing. He lay back in the grass, almost immediately falling to sleep.

■　■　■

Jeff awoke to severe disorientation. His nose nestled in the pungent scent of leather. He lifted his head and saw a neatly folded garment forming a pillow in the grass where his head had lain. It was ornately embroidered with beads. He stared at the leather garment and picked it up, letting it fall to its full size. It was a cloak. A riot of images bombarded him, most prominently, a female resembling Tami Graves wearing this very cloak. He flung the cloak to the ground backing away on his haunches and rising to his feet. "Oh, man. This is one of those dreams where you are so sure you woke up but you really didn't. You're still dreaming." He looked at his watch. It was well past the hour that had been allotted for his break. He began jogging back toward the building. "If it's still a dream, might as well get some work done." He figured that talking to himself was fine, since it was just a dream.

Before he had gone very far from the lake Lewis Henderson appeared. "Have a good nap, Jeff?" He grinned.

Jeff ignored him and kept jogging. He was fed up with this dream. Lewis merely fell into step beside him, matching his gait.

"We need you to get us into the software," Lewis said flatly.

"Wake up, Hawke!" Jeff yelled to himself.

"Tami has done it twice already, entering the hardware as a fly then changing to her energy form once inside and worming into the data stream."

"A fly?" Jeff laughed. "It's amazing how the unconscious brain mines irrelevant memories for bizarre associations." A memory he didn't realize he had surged into a vivid recall of a fly buzzing around the control room moments before a power drain and outage.

Tami joined them and jogged along the other side of him. "The second time I entered I discovered that the invaders were renegade Synons. They were much stronger than me and were about to destroy me. I reached out. You saw the image of my hand. You saved me from the renegades."

Jeff ignored the words that touched too close to raw emotions. "You cold? Want your cloak back? I left it in the grass," he snarled.

"No worry. I'm reusing its energy just now to keep up with you. You run fast. If I were human I'd be panting." They were nearing the building. "Gotta focus on imperatives right now. We must get into the system as soon as possible."

"You two? Are you a match for those babies?" Jeff grinned as if in mock complicity.

"Others are being recruited right now. We'll have a formidable force," Lewis answered him.

"Yippee!" Jeff stopped and slapped his knee. "Let the wild games begin! A fight in cyber space between globs of pure energy. Fun game!" He took off at a clip.

Lewis easily moved alongside him, grabbing his arm. "Jeff. It's not games. This is not a dream and you have to do your job."

"So, do you have a plan for how, when, and where I'm gonna get your bunch into the system? Will you be a swarm of flies? Or maybe bees?" He smiled at his own wit, illustrated by an incongruous image of computer innards overrun with a swarm of insects. How could they get inside the code itself? Maybe they copulated with the chip circuitry. He guffawed aloud.

They were at the building. "Sorry, no civilians inside." Jeff stopped and smirked.

"Tonight or tomorrow. We'll let you know what our plan is." Lewis's brow was furrowed. "Jeff, you've known me all your life. You know I'm trustworthy. I don't lie. I don't play games. The fate of the world might hinge on your cooperation. Open your heart and mind to the possibility of everything you've witnessed today. Recognize the potential of scientific theories that would validate us. Think and believe. And help."

Jeff flinched away from the penetrating eyes. "Yeah, Lew. When I wake up." Tami stepped forth and wordlessly placed a beaded bracelet on Jeff's wrist. He pulled free of Lewis's grip and strode into the building.

"You musta had a real good nap," one of the techs snarled as Jeff crept toward his station. "Man, you're covered in grass stain. Where you been anyway? Uh, you're late for a briefing. Better get in there. They were asking for you."

Jeff, still feeling very disoriented, brushed at his clothes and headed for the conference room. He had to still be dreaming. He had no recollection of waking up—but this seemed so real—so did that dream. Would he really have laid down in the grass and gone to sleep? He remembered that his intention when first going outside and walking to the lake was to get some fresh air, then take a nap in the break room that was equipped with bunk beds. Had he been so tired that he just dropped on the grass and fell into a deep sleep and its accompanying bizarre dream? He reached out to open the conference room door and noticed the beaded bracelet on his arm. Either he was still dreaming or it had all been real.

■　■　■

This tri-city area was heavily urban yet the call for Synon volunteers yielded a surprising number of local responses, and more from rural, coastal, and mountain locations.

The dearth of Passageways was not a hindrance to their quickly assembling in the Native American Cultural Center's basement, but arranging hasty and plausible reasons for a sudden absence from their human lives took some a bit of clever subterfuge and time.

Others farther away answered that they would be there as soon as they could. By late afternoon, more than fifty were milling about, getting acquainted. Giddiness rather than apprehension prevailed as they reveled in the joy of congregating with so many of their own. In a small office, Lewis, Tami, Alana, and several others were not giddy as they proposed and argued plans. Earlier, they had decided there was no alternative to confronting the renegades. Their plan was to demonstrate the numbers of Synons who stood with them and persuade the renegades to relinquish their control. They had to do what they had so often witnessed humans do: make a show of force in hopes of averting a war. Humans were usually ready and willing to fight when it became the only alternative. This group had no idea of how many renegades had infiltrated the computer system or how strong they had grown through draining energy from it and its connected components, including the municipal power source. They had to assume, despite their own hefty numbers, that they would be in a lesser position.

The fact that they were unfamiliar with this foreign environment they were about to enter, in contrast to the renegades' span of experience there, created a disparity of major proportions. They planned to leave several Synons who were strong broadcasters and receivers at the center to continue sending out pleas for volunteers and to deploy newcomers to what was understood would probably be a battlefield as they arrived. Tami had begun providing valuable instruction and practice by leading small groups into the Internet through the center's puny but adequate battery-powered system, careful to keep them away from the vicinity of the renegades. In turn, quick learners became guides for others.

Tami was grateful that Sarah had returned to the Dream Catcher. It gave her freedom.

She found a quiet time to approach Lewis Henderson. "What happened to Jeff?"

"How do you mean?"

"He obviously has a strong connection to The Living World, yet his outward behavior is crafted to display cynicism and skepticism."

"It's a complicated story. The simplified version is rather clichéd. Young Indian is steeped in tribal tradition, gets scholarship to a university, exposed to new ideas, experiences prejudice, etcetera. This one, however, had an extraordinary technology talent and developing it took him even further away."

"Cliché." She persisted, "What happened emotionally?"

Henderson shrugged. "Love, of course. What else? College sweetheart. At first, she was attracted by his heritage. Hunky Indian buck. Then she balked at meeting his family, and disdainfully rejected his marriage proposal, proclaiming that her children would be of pure European blood. Now he just says they were young and infatuated, just not right for each other."

"Why didn't his girlfriend's attitude embolden his allegiance to his heritage? Wasn't he outraged and insulted? This doesn't sound like Jeff Hawke at all."

"He is sensitive and lets few people see it. He allowed her in, and she betrayed him. He built up an emotional front, in some ways like the personas we adopt. After graduating he joined the Air Force and saw some action in the Middle East. He never talks about that. He went back to Cherokee and worked for the Tribal police for a short time before coming back here for graduate school. He stayed."

"I still don't understand human emotions." She had touched on none of this when probing Jeff's sleeping mind. He must have buried it very deep for her not to have sensed even an inkling of this early romance and betrayal. What had he experienced during his military deployment? She knew that this compartmentalization and ability to bury unwanted memories was a human coping device, but it hindered people from understanding themselves and each other.

During the busy day she thought often of calling Jeff to try persuading him to help them with their plans to confront the renegades. She knew it would be premature and could thwart their efforts. She could only hope that he came to his senses and realized the truth. They couldn't do it without his help.

CHAPTER NINE

Tami wanted to know about any "renegade" Synons, other than the extreme group that they were planning to confront.

She queried those who had answered their call, and one man called Rick said he had briefly been part of a group that had grown increasingly hostile to the Realm and other Synons. He could take her to the last place he knew they had resided. Rick warned her that it could be impossible to infiltrate them. She was willing to give it a try while they waited for their plans to be ready for implementation.

Rick led Tami to an old warehouse and manufacturing area. She considered whether to take someone with her, then decided it would be best to go alone and quickly prepared a plan. Her guide reluctantly left her, knowing if he were seen it would ruin Tami's chances of talking to them. She ventured around to the back of the boarded-up brick building where several motorcycles were parked. As she approached the door and was about to knock it swung open.

A tall, muscular man glared at her. "Whadda you want?" he demanded. She immediately reached for his mind, only to hit a wall stronger than any she'd experienced yet. Rick had warned her that this group had developed many skills.

She grinned at him. "I bet you're Bret," she cooed, her eyes roaming over his well-developed body.

"How'dya know my name?" His eyes darted about looking up and down the empty alley.

"It hasn't been easy, but I was determined. You have a bit of a rep. Won't you invite a gal in?"

"Gal?" His eyebrows rose. "I know what you are." She couldn't detect the slightest Synon essence, even a faint aura, although he apparently was able to recognize it in her.

"Good! Saves awkwardness. My persona was blown. I need a place to hide a while and rebuild it. Been asking around the right circles. Man, some of those…they're just wimps."

"Got any references?"

"Hmmm. No. I can't approach any of my former friends. Might bring wrong kind of attention to them." She dug into the large bag on her shoulder. "Here. This is an arrest record for my former self. See the mug shot?" She wore her Tami persona now, which was visible in the photo. As far as she had been able to ascertain, these Synons had never seen Tami.

"How'd you deal with—"

"Fingerprinting? I had no choice. Knocked out their power, then did a full-on total. Dropped my body. Don't think they realized what was happening. Got out, grabbing this. Thought I might need some verification. Guess I was right."

He grinned, stepped back, and opened the door. "Come on in! Welcome to our hideout."

The interior was a large loft-style living room with a long bar on one side. Closed doors were visible on the sides and back of the room. "Well, you were right, I am Bret." He motioned to a chair. "Take a load off." She sank wearily. "What'll you call yourself now?"

"Haven't decided yet. Man, what a hassle I have ahead forging a new identity." She sighed.

"We can help you there. Want a beer?" He opened a refrigerator, pulled out a bottle, jerked off the lid, and began swigging it.

"I better wait a while. This is a new body. It'll have to adjust to processing alcohol."

He eyed her appreciatively. "Well, you sure did a fantastic job with the exterior. Hot!"

She laughed. "Glad you like it. Just something I threw together."

A side door opened and a willowy blond woman emerged. She sauntered into the room, eyes glued on Tami. "So what have we here?" She stood over her. A line from one of the myriad novels she'd ingested from the Web floated in Tami's mind. "Eyes shooting daggers."

Bret moved to encircle the blond with an arm. "One of us, of course. On the lam. We can help her out a little."

Just what she needed. A jealous Synon woman. This undercover stuff might not be as easy as it seemed in all the pop culture she'd absorbed. Should she play nice or tough? "Bret kindly offered me assistance." She looked around. "Interesting place. How long you been here?"

"You don't need to know." The blond didn't move. Neither did the daggers in her eyes.

"Okay, I like it. Good vibe."

"She made a risky escape from a police station." Bret sounded almost boastful. "Had to drop her old persona and ID. Needs help setting up a new one."

The blond turned on him. "What the…you could bring 'em down on us! What if they followed her?"

"They didn't follow me." Tami stated flatly. "They couldn't see me. I cut their power, dropped my body, and got out of there. It was night; gave me cover. I got to a park where I could hide and glean energy for my new body."

Both biker Synons stared at her, something like awe in Bret's expression. These renegades had really perfected human behavior. If she didn't know better, she might entertain doubt that they were actually Synons.

The blond moved closer to him. "Bret, you forget we got a job on tonight? We need to go over plans."

He looked torn. "Yeah. We got a little time yet." He looked at Tami. "You need a name for us to call you. You can always change it later."

"Why don't you call me Tamara?"

"Okay. Now, Tamara, you'll have to get lost in a little while. Gang's all resting now; they'll be coming out for dinner soon. You can join us to eat, then leave. Sorry to throw you out so quick, but this is confidential business. We'll show you some empty buildings around here that you can stay in tonight. Then we'll catch up with you tomorrow and get you squared away."

"Sounds fine. I appreciate it. I know I just showed up on your doorstep like a lost kitten."

"Well, just chill." Bret knocked on doors, yelling, "Wake up! Time to eat!" Six people emerged from four different doors, adjusting their clothing. They all stopped and stared at Tami.

Bret made a show of telling her introduction yarn. By the end all regarded her like she was the queen she really was. She was glad she'd taken the time to concoct her story, complete with arrest report bearing a mug shot. They welcomed her, offering beer, wine, and liquor, all which she declined, citing her new body's unfamiliarity with alcohol. She was surprised at how important the meal seemed to them. Several worked at its preparation, laughing and talking as they carefully followed a recipe. They all gathered around a large wooden table, toasted their success with wine, and seemed to genuinely savor the food. She was ready to process it into energy, a task she still found a bit tedious.

"This tastes so good," a woman exclaimed. Others nodded and made full-mouth noises of assent.

Taste. Had they somehow developed that sense? How? Dare she ask? She was here to learn, so she dove in. "You've developed a sense of taste?" she asked, trying to keep her voice neutral.

"You haven't?" the blond retorted.

"I don't know anyone who has. You guys are advanced. I'm impressed." She hoped they'd share their secret with her.

"We've been here for centuries." Bret stated. "Lot of time to evolve. This came recently, when we were able to tap into scientific studies to learn how taste really works biologically and how it's transmitted to the brain. The key is the nervous system and the brain. The mind. How it perceives."

Tami tried not to gape. This was stunning information, although she'd had suspicions. Synons could evolve, tweaking their persona bodies to emulate biology. How far had others gone?

After dinner Bret and another younger man walked her a few blocks to an empty storefront. They went around to the back and pushed open an unlocked door. "You can stay here the rest of the night. We'll come by sometime tomorrow to get you." Bret kissed her cheek. "Sleep tight, Tamara." Then they were gone and she was alone with the resident mice.

They weren't as smart as they seemed. Didn't they realize she would follow them? Maybe not.

She could implement a strong mental block also, yet she had no idea how they blocked their Synon signature, and Bret had obviously recognized hers. Maybe they just assumed she had no interest in their secret "business." She reached out to Lewis Henderson, who was very strong. He suggested they use the time the bikers held their planning meeting for him to arrive at her location. He knew someone familiar with human surveillance techniques that would aid them. She found herself giggling. Just like they were in a movie.

■　　■　　■

Jeff was surprised to find that no meeting was in session in the conference room. Sitting at the far end of the otherwise empty long table were two men wearing civilian suits and grave expressions.

"Come on in, Jeff. Have a seat." One of the men greeted him in a friendly tone that didn't match his countenance. Jeff nodded and walked the length of the austere room. Its gray-green walls and gray carpet were made of sound-proof material, and the wood table and chairs added to the dark atmosphere. Normally, profuse lights embedded in the sound-proofed ceiling dispelled the dark with warm, even light; it mimicked the daylight that the lack of windows prohibited. Now, dim, strategically placed emergency lighting threw the room into splotches of light and dark.

The head of the table had room for two chairs, where the men sat. The man who had spoken was well into his middle years; his face was tunneled with wrinkles and gray hair reached almost to his shoulders. The other was quite a bit younger. In contrast to his companion, his brown hair was cut in short military style. He didn't smile; his cold blue eyes had followed Jeff from the moment he opened the door and continued to survey him as he approached them.

The friendly man beckoned to a coffee service behind him. "Have some coffee. I know you need it." A half smile cracked his face.

"Thank you," Jeff said formally. He was wary of these two and their mission. What the hell was going on? He glanced down at the bracelet Tami had placed on his wrist. Maybe I'm still dreaming, he thought.

"I'm Bailey MacIntyre, and this is Wayne Connor. We're with NSA. Go ahead and sit down, Jeff."

Jeff set his coffee on the table at a right angle to MacIntyre and took the chair in front of it. He didn't respond, waiting for an explanation. The National Security Agency would likely be interested in this situation, and might have information on the intruders, who could be from anywhere in the world—or beyond it. But why this meeting with just him? Had he unwittingly crossed some line that threw suspicion on him?

MacIntyre seemed to sense his unease. "We're working with other agencies and local authorities."

Connor interjected, "You're quite a computer whiz." Connor had a deep, growling voice. The remark did not sound like a compliment.

While uncomfortable and apprehensive, Jeff tried to remain casual. "I seem to have a knack for it. I really like my work."

"Your computer career began in the Air Force, I understand." Connor's voice and tone made it sound like an accusation.

"Yes, sir. I enlisted right after college, was well trained and appreciate it."

"You didn't want to make the military a career?"

Jeff couldn't stop a smile from curving his mouth. "I'm not the military type. Police department rules and regulations are as much as I can take." He immediately regretted his words; MacIntyre jumped in before Jeff could amend them.

"You left the military but chose law enforcement. Interesting. You could be making a bundle in private industry."

Jeff did let a small laugh escape. "The police department was about the only place back home that needed someone with my skills."

"That's right. You are Native American," Conner interjected, eyeing him.

"Yeah."

"You're sensitive about it. You started a fight with another airman over a racial slur and were reprimanded." Connor was heading somewhere, maybe not where Jeff had expected.

Jeff took the bait. "He called me an Injun hillbilly, among other things I won't repeat here. The guy made a habit of insulting minorities and women without consequences. I'd heard enough and slugged him."

MacIntyre was apparently playing good cop to Connor's bad cop. "You know, Jeff, that's the only smear we can find on your record. And we've dug deep. Believe me."

Why had they "dug deep" investigating him? A sour feeling crept through Jeff. *Here we go again. Do they think I'm a subversive and involved in the system intrusion?* He forced himself not to challenge them.

"Jeff." MacIntyre leaned closer to him. "Who do you really think is behind this cyberattack?"

Jeff tried to hide his nervousness. He wondered if he were being baited. The NSA knew everything. They probably already knew who was behind the intrusion. "They're hijacking the entire network and overwriting our operating codes and software with coding that's absolutely a mystery to us. They obviously intend to completely take command of the system. Whether they aim to expand further is still in question. Each network will have its own security protocols for them to overcome."

Connor pressed. "You still need to answer our question. Who do you think it is? Or maybe, what do you think it is?" Connor's eyebrows rose questioningly.

Jeff hedged. He picked up his coffee to take a sip, buying time. The bracelet on his wrist slid and slammed against the cup, almost tipping it over. He looked intently at the bracelet and his mind wandered. *Tami Graves an alien shape-shifter. It almost seemed logical.* His mind wandered further to the first time he saw her. His reaction had been vivid. She looked just like his adolescent dream woman. *Would such a person really exist? Had Tami, or this being she was, plucked the vision of his dream woman from his mind? If that were accepted as truth, then everything else would logically fall into place.*

"Hawke! Answer the question," Connor demanded.

"Okay." Jeff set down the cup and met Connor's eyes. He noticed MacIntyre watching intently, his expression supportive. "Okay. I've been thinking about where science and technology are going, and all the wild theories out there." He blew his breath out of his mouth. "Just thinking way outside the box. Could this be something other than normal hackers? I mean, could it be some kind of…intrusive entities?" He paused, took a deep breath and rushed on, "Whether manmade or…alien?" He looked down, afraid to view the two men's faces.

MacIntyre responded. "We've wondered the same thing, or something along the same lines. We're going to form a task force. We want you to head up the cyber investigation."

"Me? You must have the best in the business."

"We think you have an edge." MacIntyre locked eyes with him.

"I'm glad to do whatever I can," Jeff mumbled. Something about MacIntyre's look was familiar.

"I need to make a report." Connor stood up. "I'll leave you two to set this up." He strode out of the room.

Once the door had closed behind Connor, MacIntyre smiled at Jeff. "Yep," he said, nodding, "I'm one of them. A Synon. Believe me, Jeff. You are *not* dreaming. I can read your mind like a book."

Jeff gaped. His head was spinning.

"I know it's all like a dream to you, Jeff. You're human, but your bond with The Living World is as strong as ours. You are unique. We've discovered a few similar people worldwide. I think that if you really believed that you could, you would be able to telepathically communicate with us. That would be a tremendous asset."

"Is that why Tami Graves picked on me?" Disappointment and resentment mingled within Jeff.

"I think your strength simply led her to you. Try not to feel used. She genuinely cares about you."

"Oh yeah, sure. She *is* the woman of my dreams, after all." Sarcasm oozed from his voice.

"No, she's not. Enough wallowing in self-pity. We have work to do. Who in your work group do you trust the most?"

"Marie. Marie LaRue. She should have had this promotion I got; but, of course, since she's a woman, she's not a leader, according to the brass. Despite that, she's still my best friend. She always has my back."

MacIntyre smiled and nodded. "Okay. She's in. Let's go get her and blow her mind with this wild story. First, let me fill you in on a little more about us." Jeff sat transfixed as MacIntyre told him about the Realm, Passageways between their two universes and the long history between humans and the Synons who sought to protect The Living World. "It sounds fantastic, I know. I think in your heart you understand."

■　　■　　■

As Tami sat pondering these "renegade" Synons a new Synon presence appeared in her mind telling her that he was Lew Henderson's friend and was coming in, not to attack him.

A fit middle-aged man with long gray hair immediately entered and introduced himself as Bailey MacIntyre, a Synon living as a long-time National Security Agency agent. "We only have tonight," he announced. "Today I met your friend Jeff. He's still kind of in shock but I got through to him. He'll lead our Cyber Unit. Now about this rogue bunch. I've heard of them. I'm curious about this job they have tonight. It might be a chance to find out what they're up to. I assumed they'd take off on their bikes, so I parked the one I borrowed on the next street over where we can easily hide in an alley between buildings until we hear them pass. If they don't use their bikes, they would have to walk since there's no public transportation around here." One of his bushy eyebrows rose. "And it's unlikely that a ride share driver would venture into a neighborhood like this, especially after dark." So he had mastered humor.

MacIntyre was right. Four motorcycles zoomed past their alley, each carrying two passengers. As soon as the bikes turned a corner, the two Synons jumped on theirs and sped off. It was an exhilarating experience for Tami. MacIntyre was adept at maintaining a safe distance while keeping the prey in sight. They followed through suburbs into a rural area, taillights in the distance like blinking red eyes. Not needing illumination, MacIntyre turned his lights off, keeping a discreet distance behind. On the right was a broad open area, punctuated by a line of high-tension electric towers. In the darkness the two Synons could perceive the electromagnetic field dancing around them. The bikes swerved off the road into the field, parking a short distance from the towers, within a small grove of trees.

MacIntyre parked on the side of the road some distance away; he and Tami dismounted and crept forward. They saw eight human forms approach the towers and begin to climb. As they did so, brilliant auras surrounded them. It was hard to perceive exactly what they were doing as they reached the insulated supports; then the sky lit up with myriad bolts of lightning that abruptly faded, while the eight figures looked like pulsating masses of lightning. They were stealing power and somehow containing it. Clearly no longer material forms, the masses descended and floated into the woods beyond.

MacIntyre and Tami had no choice but to shed their own personas, hoping that their significant auras wouldn't attract attention. They could remain relatively far behind since their prey was so brilliant. Obviously, there were no residents nearby. They swept deep into the silent forest, startled and terrified creatures fleeing in their wake. Time had no measure. A nearly full moon was rising in the east, casting its own glow. The eight globules stopped at the edge of a rocky pool formed by a tall waterfall. Within this environment, even with the fright the intruders instilled, Nature's presence was pervasive. How ironic that such a place existed in such close proximity to the towering symbols of humanity's efforts to wrench Nature's power from her.

Just before the eight coalesced into one blinding bulk, Tami and MacIntyre linked onto a Passageway nestled behind the falls. The mass of Synon current flew toward its pulsating perimeter, surrounding it. The brilliant ring that formed around the Passageway began gradually moving inward. They were closing the Passageway! MacIntyre and Tami, two of the most powerful individual Synons of the Realm, knew they were no match for that astounding aggregation of power. They could only hover and observe as the direct link to the Realm grew dimmer, and with it the mass of power, now nearly spent in the monumental effort. A person would not have been aware of the eight entities housed in minute swaths of current, each struggling to regain its integrity.

"They're severely weakened now," MacIntyre telepathed. "Let's confront them."

Calling on ambient life for strength, they expanded into amorphous pulsating rainbows of energy, each of them almost rivaling that so recently displayed by any one of the eight that now were trying unsuccessfully to flit away.

"Abominations!" MacIntyre's voice boomed in their minds. "You have brought on the wrath of TuMa'Aye Gra'Vay, Queen of the Realm!" The two powerful beings loomed over the tiny eight.

Bret's voice weakly echoed in their minds. "You fooled me. Heard rumors you were here, just never believed you'd bother leaving your exalted perch."

"I speak for The Living World. I go where I'm most needed and do what is most needed to be done." TuMa'Aye Gra'Vay's voice reverberated with authority and power. "I can understand the desire to remain and live as humans, but not to risk severing Earth's lifeline to the Realm."

"Just like people. Enjoy it while we can. Use our power to adjust and evolve, seek new paths."

TuMa'Aye was intrigued. "So you harbor some optimism? Does that include for Earth's biological inhabitants?"

"Don't know. Renegades all over the world are working on different things."

"Are they trying to help people and other of Earth's life?"

"Maybe. People might just be dooming it all." A pause. "I'm getting too weak to communicate. Can you help us get back to our personas?"

MacIntyre's voice rang out. "I prefer to reopen that Passageway and send you all to the Realm."

He and TuMa'Aye felt a negative torrent and a barely imperceptible response. "That would be torture. Been here too long."

TuMa'Aye was decisive. "We won't give you the power for human form. You'll be small creatures but can still talk to us." She and MacIntyre directed focused power to the eight whose miniscule amorphous life forces shimmered. In a few moments, eight rabbits sat in front of the re-formed personas of MacIntyre and Tami. "You're cute little things. However, not all people will think so. Some will enjoy hunting you, as will birds of prey and other predators. You'll understand the stage of evolution at which animal life on Earth exists now."

Waves of terror emanated from the rabbits.

TuMa'Aye's voice carried a touch of compassion. "It will take you some time to gain sufficient power to change to larger creatures, but quite a while to form human personas again. You will feel a vibrant link to The Living World. Grasp it, learn, and reflect. If you decide you want to return to the Realm, reach out to me. I will always hear you." She looked around the moonlit forest. "Your instincts will lead you in this bountiful ecosystem. Be safe and take care of each other." She turned and walked away, followed by MacIntyre. Eight bunnies huddled together in the moonlight.

TuMa'Aye didn't tell the renegades that she planned to visit them very soon. She also didn't relate that she was speaking to nearby predators admonishing them not to hunt the eight rabbits. They were one small renegade group, yet she could learn a great deal from them about their development over the centuries.

Knowledge that could aid her and her allies in the monumental task ahead of reaching out to renegades all over the world.

■　■　■

A small delegation to the Realm had left for Passageways still open in the mountains. In their far-reaching history, the very idea of Synons slaying one another did not exist. These events on Earth would be the most devastating the Synons had ever witnessed. TuMa'Aye Gra'Vay was torn. She felt that her presence was needed in the Realm to help them accept this catastrophic news that was creating turmoil there, despite Tork's efforts; yet she knew that she must remain to lead the Synons against the renegades.

■　■　■

In the government War Room, as it was dubbed, Jeff and Marie were ecstatic as they surveyed the array of electronic equipment. It was indeed a war room, hidden deep underground, heavily shielded and protected, and impressively provisioned. A facility no one ever suspected rested beneath a typical federal office building.

Marie had acclimated quickly to the mind-boggling situation. Her reactions had been matter of fact as she ticked off scientific theories that supported the outrageous story she had been told about energy beings from another universe who traveled to Earth via "Passageways" which she deemed were wormholes. Jeff found her presence comforting as they mingled with the

other task force members; they were all from various government agencies, a few revealing that they were Synons.

MacIntyre, who had coordinated with the Synon contingent,
entered. "Please welcome our Synon partners." The Synons uncer-
emoniously sauntered in, wearing their recognizable human personas, some grinning, others awkward and shy, and still others
stern-faced. Tami Graves stepped to the front as the Synons
formed a group in the center of the room. When he saw her, Jeff
felt a flush wash over his face. She looked serenely at him.

"Hi Jeff."

He heard only the normal Tami voice he was used to.

"I'm so very glad you're our tech leader," TuMa'Aye
Gra'Vay's voice intoned. "You have the strength we need."

He knew his face was beet red now. He could only dip his
head and mutter, "Thanks." Beside him, Marie gently punched
his arm. "Uh, Tami, this is my colleague and friend, Marie."

■　　■　　■

The two women nodded at each other, and Tami smiled
warmly at Marie. "I'm really glad Jeff has a friend like you by his
side." Marie visibly swallowed and smiled wanly.

Tami hoped that Jeff would realize that Marie was his
true soul mate and the personality on which Tami was based,
melded with his adolescent vision of the perfect woman. She
knew Marie was the real "woman of his dreams." Wistfulness
engulfed Tami, filling her with a sense of loss for the attachment
she had formed to Jeff, one she knew could never be the kind
of relationship humans enjoyed. She sighed and straightened
herself. Duty called.

"Let's just take a few minutes to all get acquainted," Tami said. A sense of exhilaration prevailed as human and Synon colleagues openly greeted each other. For the Synons present, who now outnumbered the humans, it was a welcome relief to be among people who knew what they were and gladly accepted them.

"Now," Tami's voice rang out over the hubbub. "Time for work. We need to hammer out a plan." She sat cross-legged on the floor. "Please join me. We need a true brainstorming session." Furniture was moved around to create an open space on the carpet. Soon everyone sat together except a few humans glued to dark computer monitors that at any instant could spark a clue to the renegades.

The exchange was surprisingly orderly. Multiple people spoke simultaneously only a few times, and no one tried to shout down others. There was no intelligence on how far across the networking systems the renegades had disbursed or the extent of their numbers and strength. The Task Force was fairly certain that they had not gone beyond the extended municipal network, including local utilities, which had all now been shut down. The only energy source the renegades had was the vast reservoir they had stored within themselves.

There was a lengthy, sometimes heated, discussion among the Synon force about how to approach the renegades. A straightforward plan was initially put forth in which the TFS, Task Force Synons, as they had been designated, would deploy in groups at the network's outer perimeters and work their way inward. There was data on the isolated spots that had been displaying energy bursts and were assumed to be renegade locations; these were the initial targets.

The tactics for engaging the renegades when they were directly met was the major source of argument. All of the Synons were loath to consider trying to destroy another Synon. They didn't even know how to accomplish that act other than the way the renegades had apparently done to others like the Jordans, by simply absorbing their energy. An abhorrent suggestion. Most insisted there had to be a way to communicate, persuade them to stand down and rejoin the Realm. That was what Tami had initially assumed would be their strategy. The question was raised of how to go about it without being annihilated in the process. They needed a way to disable the renegades. To drain their power. They decided to implement the initial plan to search for renegades who might be hibernating.

■　■　■

Darkness swallowed what was normally a metropolitan area brilliant with light. The War Room was eerily bright from generators that also powered independent computers connected to outside security and communications networks. External communications systems had also been established for all emergency services. All computers within the greater municipal network were left essentially dead. No generator power had been allowed in the network system for hours.

"They might not be as smart as we think they are," Marie mused as she and Jeff sat down at their stations. "They've gobbled up the city network, in the process robbing themselves of the power they need to continue. What can they be doing in there? How long will their batteries last?" She smirked at her own wit. "I know, they can amass and hold huge quantities of power, but where?"

"I just know that they were like masses of energy when I encountered them. You're right, though. I was working deep in software code. Maybe they're asleep."

"I just wish I could see the fireworks when our guys meet them."

"You mean our Task Force Synons?"

"Of course. The good guys. Our White Hats."

He chuckled. "I'm amazed at how you've adjusted to all this."

She gave him a look he'd never seen from her. "Well, I'm actually relieved that the gorgeous Tami isn't really human. Who could compete with that?" She locked eyes with him.

Jeff, flooded with confusing feelings, broke eye contact. Was Marie jealous? That possibility brought surprise and joy. What was she saying? He looked at her. She was beautiful in a pixie way with her short blond hair and delicate bone structure. He suddenly felt shy. It was nothing like the shyness he'd felt with Tami, who had seemed to be so much out of his league that her attention had made him feel like a teenager experiencing his first crush. Marie smiled at him and he thought he might be blushing, not like a teenager, but a man astonished that this extraordinary woman might be in love with him and that he felt the same way. The thought was astounding. How long had he loved Marie? How could he have suppressed it?

Jeff tried to think back through their relationship. There had immediately been a warm rapport between them. They talked and joked easily. He felt comfortable with her. He never felt she was judging him. She was always there supporting him. He regarded her as his best friend. He took her for granted. What a jerk he was. She was too close. Too comfortable. Not exotic or exciting. Yet, when he looked at her now he saw what many men would regard as an exotic, exciting woman. He had buried it. He had developed techniques for burying feelings he didn't want to acknowledge. Now he could recognize that she had given him signs that his barriers made him ignore. Soothing touches when he was troubled. Looks. Never intention-ally seductive, rather, warm and affectionate. There was no rule in their job categories that prevented a personal relationship yet his own need to retain walls, maintaining the unencumbered life he had built, kept him shut off. He hadn't even acquired a pet despite his love of animals. He didn't have to acknowledge this at all to Marie. He didn't have to let her know how he really felt about her. But now that he had recognized it could he keep ignoring it? Go on as usual? Thoughts rushed through his mind the way the renegade code had scrolled on his computer screen. What seemed like minutes was seconds. Seconds in which his life had changed.

Marie smoothly returned to the conversation about the White Hats. "I wish I could be a little fly watching it all when they go in there." They both laughed in their comfortable way.

He sobered, mind reverting to the crisis at hand. "The White Hats want to avoid battle. Their weapon has to be persuasion."

CHAPTER TEN

TuMa'Aye Gra'Vay allowed herself to luxuriate in the glory of being pure energy only for a moment before gliding into the server labyrinth. She felt the exhilaration of those who followed and hurriedly sent them warning messages to maintain self-control. She then began broadcasting a steady, calm message. We are your family. We want to help you. We won't harm you. Meet us outside so that we can resolve this peacefully. Her broadcast continued as she floated, amplified by those behind her. Others were echoing the same message within perimeter routes, all forming a converging path that would end in the heart of the system's vast network. They were all met with silence. No sign of the renegades.

Maybe their power enables them to continue working within the software, TuMa'Aye mused to herself. They had assumed that without continuous power, the renegades were simply hibernating, perhaps in hardware or cables, conserving energy, venturing into software only for those short bursts that had been detected. Could she and some of the strongest of her group muster the power to do the same? She had to attempt it. She exited and appeared in the War Room as Tami Graves, to the surprise of those working there. She approached Jeff. "Is it possible to switch on the system long enough for me and several others to get into the software code where the renegades have been?"

For a minute, Jeff just stared at her. She was so matter of fact. His mind was sketching a hilarious image of Tami Graves crawling into a computer motherboard and skittering along, skating on silicon chips, trying to break into them. "We could try it." Mirth was replaced by the memory of his brief encounter with the renegades. "I just hope you have enough power to do what you plan, if they're there."

"I'm going with you." Bailey MacIntyre strode out of the glassed office where he had been manning communications. "I am very strong." Tami nodded and proceeded to gather the rest of her team.

Jeff booted up his unit and logged onto the network. Error messages appeared. He drilled down into the operating system coding that was now populated entirely by foreign script. "Okay, Tami," he said into his communications device. "It's running. Good luck, little flies."

"Jeff, before I transform, I must urge you to make every effort to connect with me telepathically. I know you can do it. We need your guidance in there."

"Now?"

"Whenever." He heard Tami's familiar sardonic tone and chuckled. He realized suddenly how much she reminded him of Marie. A thought he tucked away to ponder later.

Jeff's attention immediately turned to the screen. "Game on," he whispered, fighting a sense of inadequacy. Could he replicate that moment when he and what he recognized had been Tami's hands had touched in cyberspace?

Tami had brought only ten Synons with her, fearing it was a suicide mission, a bizarre notion for those from the Realm. She had perfected the feat of entering miniscule openings in hardware connections as a fly, transforming into an energy form, then locating and worming her way into the internal avenues of software and synchronizing with them. It didn't take long for her to lead her team into the software itself. They were fast learners and had practiced this maneuver. But their practice runs had not prepared them for what they encountered. Like a blizzard, knots of power pummeled them from all sides. Surges of malice assaulted their minds. They began to fight for their lives.

■　　■　　■

Jeff had closed his eyes and, despite the terror it elicited, tried to immerse himself in the environment of his encounter with the renegades when he had rescued Tami. Instead, images from childhood floated in his mind's eye.

A powwow gathering of several Native American tribes. He was in a sweat lodge. He had effortlessly drifted into a trance-like state, while his buddies giggled and remained unfazed. Instinctively, his psyche now yielded to a similar dreamlike state. Abruptly he was in the software. Just ahead of his location he saw vibrant pulsating energy. Opposing forces of emotion battered him: a warm, glowing, serene feeling of oneness punctuated by nefarious hostility. He reached for Tami who welcomed him with a small portion of her attention and clamped onto him as if grasping for a lifeline. She was struggling to retain her autonomy amid an enemy onslaught. Jeff held fast to her, channeling all his being into the bond. He couldn't help her fight, but he could help her survive.

■   ■   ■

Marie felt rather than saw Jeff's transformation. She reached over and clasped his hand. It was apparent that he was in a trancelike state. She felt isolated and ineffective yet knew it was vital to maintain contact with him. They stayed that way for what seemed an interminable time. She felt like screaming. She forced herself to relax and practice the meditative techniques she often employed during stressful situations. Gradually she relaxed, experiencing the comfort of closeness with Jeff.

Jeff had barely mentioned Tami to her, but she knew that in the last few days he had been preoccupied with more than the cyber incursion. She guessed that it was Tami he had met for dinner after a furtive phone conversation. Marie had felt a pang of what she had to admit was jealousy. By the time she laid eyes on Tami Graves Marie knew that she was not what she appeared to be. Tami's remarkable beauty had to have effected Jeff. Marie wondered how he was really coping with the revelation that this exquisite woman wasn't human. He had to be in turmoil. The way she had just blurted out that remark about Tami being unfair competition should have embarrassed her, yet the way Jeff had looked at her had silently acknowledged the affection between them. She basked in a warm glow.

All these thoughts rested quietly in the recesses of Marie's mind. Her focus was on maintaining a connection with Jeff. She stretched her mind to imagine—if not actually grasp—the extended connections. At first, all she could envision was flies flitting around inside cables and hardware. Gradually it was feelings rather than imagery that brought a sensation of glowing strands of connection. Jeff began to twitch and twist. His jaw was clenched and his muscles visibly tensed. Marie instinctively knew that the White Hats had not been met peacefully. She held tighter to Jeff's hand.

■　■　■

Tami felt her team struggle to maintain their psychic link as she sent them urgent messages to stay together and form a phalanx behind her.

Jeff's surprisingly potent connection resonated through her and she felt Marie anchoring him to the real world. It was like a delicate string pulsating amid tumult.

She marshaled strength to speak to the renegades. "We don't want war. We want to understand why you are doing this. If you stand down, we will too. This is not the Synon way."

A rush of energy pummeled her, accompanied by the same voice from the attack at the pond. "We are no longer Synons. We are a new species. We have no interest in you other than absorbing your energy." Another barrage flung her backward. Her companions buffered her as best they could. The voice continued. "You're just trying to dissipate our energy. Get out or be destroyed."

MacIntyre spoke. "We're curious about how you accomplished all this."

A new, sarcastic tone crept into the renegade's response. "Wanna join us? Well, I think not."

"How did you evolve? What's your objective?"

"I will control everything." A new volley struck the team, slamming them back farther.

MacIntyre persisted. "How? All you control right now is one city's computer network and power generation. One city among thousands on this Earth. You're destroying the very information stream you want to be your new kingdom. You need to rethink your plans. You've been here immersed in your own fantasies too long."

"You can't dislodge me. I'll evolve and find new ways to achieve what I want." As before, his declaration was accompanied by an onslaught of energy.

As MacIntyre engaged the renegade in conversation Tami had been assessing the situation. The renegade's army had retreated far behind him. They took no initiative. It seemed that the brunt of the attacks had come directly from the leader. How much power did he really have left? Maybe they could keep goading him into squandering it in futile displays. Maybe they could overcome him.

A quick acknowledgment from MacIntyre sparked in her mind. He had gotten her message and agreed with it. He moved forward a bit. "You know, I've gotten kind of used to communicating as Bailey MacIntyre. I really wish I could talk to you man to man out there in the real world."

"I don't bite. And I'm tired of impersonating humans. I am already a new species."

MacIntyre's tone grew commanding, "You forget the power of the Realm. We can formulate a kind of energy force that will contain you. Once we drag you out of this false utopia the power you've accumulated will disperse rapidly, especially if you're surrounded by innumerable Synons and herded through a Passageway. You might be strong now in your little enclave, but the mass of Synons now forming here and in the Realm can easily contain you. You'd best consider your options carefully." He was answered by a renewed attack.

Alana abruptly detached from the tight formation behind Tami and disappeared. The environment became charged with turbulence. Particles of matter swirled, coalescing around the renegades. Alana was disrupting the physical material around them. Tami and MacIntyre reacted swiftly, leading their group to rescue Alana, but Alana was gone. A faint residue of her essence emanated from the renegade leader. Alana had been absorbed.

■　　■　　■

The jangle of a phone invaded the tranquil state Marie had achieved. It seemed to come from far away, and it insistently continued ringing. Why hadn't someone answered it? Marie surveyed the area. She and Jeff were the only people in the open computer section. The few others in the War Room were in separate glass offices, intent on their tasks. Marie realized the ringing was from a cell phone that lay on the desk next to Jeff's computer, which she recognized wasn't his. She picked it up. The caller ID read: "Dr. Gabe Jackson." "Hello?" she answered.

A smooth male voice spoke. "Have they had enough?"

"What?" Marie glanced over at Jeff. He sat motionless, eyes clenched.

Her attention returned to the phone. "Who is this? Who are you calling?"

"Can Miss Graves please come to the phone?" The tone was oily and mocking. "I called her number. Is she busy?" He cackled.

"You're calling Tami Graves?"

The voice turned sharp. "Put the phone's earpiece in Jeff's ear. Not a request."

"Just a minute." Marie complied, also pressing the speaker button on the phone so that she could hear.

"Can you hear me, Queenie?" The voice oozed derision. Jeff's body jerked, his eyes remaining closed. "Fancy me, that mischievous ole rascal Bandela transformed into the mighty renegade leader. You thought I was too weak to navigate a Passageway. Well, guess what? I did!" His voice rose on the last word, dragging it out. "Hut to! Renegade Army, back off a minute so I can converse with Queenie."

    ■   ■   ■

TuMa'Aye Gra'Vay, Queen of the Realm, felt the malicious energy field that had gripped her loosen. Bandela. The last Synon she would ever have suspected of leading the renegades. He continued, voice routed through the earpiece and Jeff's connection to her. "You didn't return my call," he said pouting.

"What call?"

"My persona is Dr. Gabe Jackson. You asked for an appointment to interview me. I left a message to arrange it."

"Oh, oh yes. The biomechanics expert. Well, Bandela, or rather, Dr. Jackson, if I'd known it was you, I'd certainly have made every effort to meet with you. Congratulations on your accomplishments." She noted that the renegade attack had not diminished. Bandela was demonstrating his strength and capabilities. Taunting, bragging, but also intimidating as he conducted simultaneous activities.

He replied, "I wanted to gloat, of course. To brag to you. I really have achieved a lot. For instance, I learned that technology is far superior to biology."

"I see that. Extremely impressive, Gabe; may I call you that? Could we meet somewhere outside and converse? How about the park with the globe fountain at its center?" She referred to the same park where she had first met Cat and subsequently been whisked away with the homeless in a police raid that ultimately brought her to this moment. Bandela was inconsistent. He had declared his disdain for human pursuits, but now seemed to enjoy boasting about his persona's accomplishments. Maybe he was wavering. That presented a possible way to get him out.

He quickly bristled. "You want to draw me out of my fortification so that you can try to imprison or destroy me?"

"I want a truce. I want us to find ways to coexist without you harming people."

"I kind of like harming people. And the *pièce de résistance*, absorbing Synons."

All traces of conciliation were gone as the Queen of the Realm declared, "Bandela, as we speak, a delegation of Earth-dwelling Synons is discussing this situation in the Realm. They know where the open Passageways are. You might be formidable, but do not doubt the force you will soon face. We are allied with The Living World. Your game is over. Give us the chance to save you and your followers."

The phone connection abruptly ended as the renegade launched a renewed attack on the TFS. As he battered them his voice resounded. "I will soon control this entire planet, maybe more. Why would I even consider negotiating with you?"

The regal voice of TuMa'Aye Gra'Vay reverberated. "For that very reason. The Living World will not allow your abomination. You'd be wise to deal with the Realm now. Although Synons do not destroy their own kind, The Living World protects itself. Do not think that you can create your own universe."

"We'll see about that." His attempt to scoff betrayed traces of misgiving. He knew the TFS wouldn't give up.

As the battle quieted momentarily the material world in which they were encased demonstrated its capabilities for chaos. The detritus from Alana's disruption of the surrounding material sparked into combustion from the intense energy bursts of the Synon battle. Flames snaked through the hardware like a fire-breathing dragon. The hardware in which they were encased was burning, separating the opposing forces. TuMa'Aye Gra'Vay broadcast an urgent message to Jeff to send all Synons from the War Room into the server room immediately, along with fire-fighters with fire suppression equipment. She hoped to contain the renegades as they were forced to exit the conflagration but her priority was saving her own. Just outpacing encroaching flames, the TFS backtracked in search of an exit point.

Fortunately, the sprinkler system was on back-up power and was spraying water inside the server room as it filled with smoke. This made it hard to pinpoint where the fire was, so those manning extinguishers began spraying all the stacked rows of equipment. Suddenly they were all knocked to the floor, trampled by what looked like a huge elephant that was untouched by the smoke and water. The renegades had emerged and taken advantage of the situation, coalescing to become a beast. The Synons sprang to action, transforming into saber-toothed tigers and other large predators that attacked the rampaging creature, providing an opportunity for the humans to escape. Despite inflicting numerous injuries, they failed to bring the beast down. The creature raised its trunk and ripped off a ceiling air vent enclosure. In the murk a large, apish creature appeared and easily leapt into the vent. Synons transformed into various creatures and took chase. By then the TFS had emerged and joined the pursuit, but the renegades had disappeared.

When the pandemonium subsided and the fire was under control, a council was called in the War Room.

■   ■   ■

The conflict with the renegades had been short but deadly. Four Synons had been absorbed, including the intense young Alana, who had fought so valiantly. Several people hurt in the melee were treated by the attendant medical staff. Although devastated by the loss, TuMa'Aye Gra'Vay was grateful that both MacIntyre and Henderson had survived.

When she emerged Jeff reacted. "Are we stupid or what? All this time, we could have just burned them out."

Tami was grim. "It wasn't planned. She told them of Alana's tactic that inadvertently resulted in the fire.

A somber mood hovered until Jeff's tone changed. "Who the hell was that anyway?"

Marie joined in. "Yeah, who...?"

Tami smiled affectionately. This resilient curiosity was one of her favorite human traits.

"Bandela, a Synon I would never have expected to be on Earth, much less the powerful leader he's become."

"Powerful is right," Jeff interrupted. "He was in the network software and at the same time was able to link to your cell phone."

"Bandela was thought too ineffective to navigate Passageways." As she spoke, everyone who wasn't occupied with tasks drifted over to listen. The humans were especially fascinated. As past events replayed in her memory, Tami summarized them for her audience. She was an adept storyteller.

■　　■　　■

The Synon battle reverberated through the Realm, which became so turbulent that its residents were at risk of dissolution. Only the extreme efforts of Tork held them together until the renegades had escaped and some semblance of stasis emerged.

"We must learn from our mistakes," he telepathed. "Let's join and calmly review what we know of Bandela." The agitated Synons struggled to follow his directions. The review played out in their collective mind.

It had been some time in the past. None could pinpoint how long ago. They recalled a single Synon who had begun to assert himself, role-playing as a swashbuckling human pirate. He was arrogant, seeking to dominate conversations and boasting of his strength and ability to emulate humans. His neighbors were tolerant. They had witnessed similar behavior before in those new to visiting Earth and trying to build their confidence. But Bandela persisted, recreating his image in the mold of a venerated prophet, wearing magnificent robes and carrying a jeweled staff. He became officious and even called a conclave at which he declared that he was establishing an archive of the Realm's deliberations, decisions, and actions. He was to be referred to as the Archivist, not Bandela. That pronouncement was dismissed, again, with some knowing humor, as just another novice's attempt to mimic humans. Such an undertaking could not be implemented in the Realm; maintaining such voluminous records would require impossible amounts of energy. Bandela moved to a new phase, unobtrusively going about his work for a while; then he returned to making officious intrusions into the Realm's affairs. He would seize control of gatherings and scold them on past errors he had uncovered. He was disregarded and eventually grew comical as he became less able to control his persona. He could never hold that image long, reverting to what appeared to be a default authentic persona: a portly, sneering codger with a snout-like nose resembling that of a pig.

■　　■　　■

"That kind of humiliation could generate some simmering rage," Marie interjected as Tami's narrative, paralleling that unfolding in the Realm, paused.

Tami nodded. "He began to retreat into seclusion for longer periods. We didn't even notice when he left. I think we were just glad to be rid of his disruption and were relieved by his absence. In time, no one thought to question it. Now we deal with the consequences." She sighed audibly. "Synons, let's all send mental messages to Bandela to meet us in the park tonight. I think he might be ready to face us, although he could arrive ready for a new fight. If he thinks about his options, he'll realize that it's only a matter of time until he's contained by a superior force." She paused, then turned to face her human partners. "Jeff, Marie. I want you to go with me, MacIntyre, and Henderson to meet Bandela."

"Us? The fate of humanity is at stake and we'll be its representatives?" Jeff blurted.

"Would Mulder and Scully balk?" Tami's sardonic quip reminded them that they were witnessing a dual personality. TuMa'Aye Gra'Vay was Queen of the Realm, but Tami Graves ruled here, like Marie, displaying her penchant for vintage television like the classic "X Files." The comment embedded a subtle comparison to its male and female investigative duo whose up and down relationship took several seasons to finally cross into the romantic.

CHAPTER ELEVEN

Jeff and Marie's flashlights threw narrow ribbons of illumination as they journeyed through the park that lay cloaked in a black shroud.

With no aura of city lights, the sky should have glittered with stars, but a low swath of clouds intensified the darkness. The Synons leading the way didn't seem hindered by the dark as they silently wound along the path. As they neared the central fountain with its towering sculptural centerpiece, a shard of moon appeared like a slit in an ebony curtain. It glinted off the tall bronze globe suspended on supports jutting out of the fountain. The globe represented the Earth. It all seemed eerily unreal to Jeff. As they approached the fountain, the atmosphere was charged with menacing power. Jeff shivered; he instinctively knew the renegades were there. His arm involuntarily encircled Marie, drawing her closer. A dazzling display of lightning lit up the sky, followed by a thunderclap that reverberated as a phantom sauntered toward them, revealing a very human-looking tall, fit figure.

"Well, here I am! Like the look, Queenie?" He twirled like a runway model. "I aimed for a distinguished, debonair aspect, with a dash of the rakish." He winked.

Tami, Henderson, and MacIntyre moved to meet him, motioning their companions to remain where they were. Jeff glanced at Marie, and as one, they also stepped forward, leaving their small Synon escort behind. Tami had asked them to accompany her, Henderson, and MacIntyre, and that's what they'd do. Jeff had been in dangerous situations before but thought this was probably the most frightening in Marie's life. It was certainly the strangest for both of them. He tamped down his fear, focusing on their surroundings. He knew the Synons they stood with had power he could not imagine and had to trust that they would protect them.

Tami gave the dapper gentleman a haughty once over. "Very good. I'm glad you agreed to join us. Now we can converse in a civilized manner. You've proven that you are extremely capable on the human plane." Jeff had never experienced Tami this way. She exuded confident superiority, but her tone was conversational, even complimentary. "Perhaps you would consider continuing Dr. Jackson's illustrious career. Your work on computerized prosthetics has benefited many human amputees. That is probably just the beginning for you."

Bandela-Jackson strolled closer, eyeing the five figures before him, then circled them, throwing menacing glances their way as he prattled. "Your flattery is so transparent. And so patronizing." His tone grew pompous. "Yes, yes. I have demonstrated my ability to con The Living World into letting me through a Passageway, then passing myself off as a human for years, achieving success and renown. I have more than proven myself to both the Realm and humanity. I could go on and prob-ably win a Nobel Prize, but it has all become so boring. I crave more stimulation. I want to know it all, experience it all." He locked threatening eyes with Tami's. "Control it all."

"How can you mock The Living World so?" Lewis Henderson's deep voice resonated. "You could not have conned your way through a Passageway. Your Synon essence was linked to The Living World enough to get here. You will never be able to discard that essence. And The Living World will control you."

Jeff was dumbfounded. He had known Lew Henderson much of his life and was still struggling to digest the startling revelation that he was an otherworldly being. Now he witnessed his laconic friend intimidating a monster.

Bandela-Jackson ignored the threats. "I am unique. Nothing controls me. My plan gestated long ago and has evolved beautifully." He pranced and boasted with grandiose gestures, momentarily forgetting to be menacing, lost in his own self-aggrandizement. "My work as archivist in the Realm provided me with so much data on human behavior. It was fun to frolic around the Realm mimicking people, but I wanted to be one. I led an exciting double life here too. Staid scientist by day, renegade leader by night. Even that got boring. The 'renegades,'"—he tweaked two fingers in the air—"are mostly a sham. I do all the blustering. All the absorbing. They're just along for the ride. Bored like me. Looking for some excitement, but they're puny Synons beside the commanding power I have amassed."

Henderson persisted. "Exactly how did you amass all that power?"

Bandela-Jackson's eyes glinted in the moonlight like glit-tering knives. He glided around the group peering at each one as if about to shout "boo!" "People are obsessed with all their amenities, appliances, gadgets. All requiring power. It's so easy to scoop up bits of it here and there. I tire of humans." The sinister tone returned. "They are even weaker than my renegade companions."

MacIntyre spoke up. "Bandela, you are an abomination, yet you aren't the first Synon to feel the stress of trying to compress our expansive beings into impersonating these imperfect creatures. After all, they are still early in their evolution. But you abandoned the very source that can help you." As MacIntyre lectured, Bandela-Jackson continued circling the group, radiating malice. Jeff's sense of danger heightened. He and Marie were the only humans witnessing this alien confrontation.

Bandela-Jackson continued his threatening posturing, drawing close to each of his adversaries in turn, sparks now and then darting from his raised fingertips. MacIntyre ignored the performance, simply turning to face Bandela-Jackson as his position changed, continuing to expound. "I've spent a lot of time here and could not have continued without making occasional excursions to the Realm. It clarifies my objective and replenishes me. Soon I need to get back to the hands-on work of protecting The Living World through the nitty-gritty existence of my human alter ego. It would take a very long time to tell you all the terrible things I've helped avert as Bailey MacIntyre. I know that in time, he'll have to pass on. Then I'll refresh myself in the Realm and eventually return to Earth and take on another identity that can serve The Living World."

Bandela-Jackson stopped in front of MacIntyre, laser-like eyes boring into him. "Well, bully for you. I just don't care about serving The Living World. In fact, I'm not sure it exists. I think maybe the Realm is just another universe accessible through wormholes. Maybe I should go back there and seek paths to other universes where beings are more advanced." His expression changed. "Ah, that would be no fun if they had already progressed too far for me to influence their world."

Henderson, visibly irritated with MacIntyre's tactic, cornered Bandela-Jackson, standing close to him, eye to eye. "What happens to the Synons you absorb?" he growled.

The sarcastic, mocking tone returned. "Ah. Well, it is true. Synons can't destroy other Synons. They just kind of go 'poof' and become part of the stronger ones who are pulling them apart. They get absorbed."

"Do they continue to exist as individual entities within another Synon?"

"Unfortunately, they do. And they can become pests. It took me a long time to learn how to suppress them."

Jeff was so startled that he forgot he was just an observer. He broke in. "So every Synon you've ever absorbed is still essentially alive? Can you let them out?"

"Let them out? Why would I want to do that?" Bandela-Jackson had moved away back toward the fountain.

Marie was also excited by this revelation and blurted, "They would no longer pester you. You wouldn't have to expend energy suppressing them."

"But they would turn on me. Seek revenge."

"Bandela, revenge is purely human. You need a reset." MacIntyre shook his head in dismay. "You need to go back to the Realm and contemplate. Ponder where you went wrong and how you can right yourself."

Now Jeff was irritated. "Oh no. He's not getting off so easy." He addressed Bandela-Jackson directly. "You wrecked a city's vital computer networks, closed down its utilities, and brought it to a standstill. If you want to reform yourself, start by cleaning up your mess. Give us back our systems."

"I haven't agreed to reform." Bandela-Jackson was petulant. "I did you a big favor. That code can upgrade your system's capabilities beyond what you could do in a lifetime."

"Well, we can't read it. It's useless to us." Jeff's outrage overshadowed his squeamish reaction to direct eye contact with the renegade Synon.

MacIntyre played the appeaser. "This is where I can help. Very few people are aware of this mystery code. It must remain classified. We'll develop a cover story for how it got into the system and then reshape Jackson. We'll present him as a computer whiz working for the NSA who has broken the code and figured out how to repair your systems."

"That might be fun," Bandela-Jackson mused.

"Then Dr. Jackson goes on an extended sabbatical and you, Bandela, go to the Realm and contemplate your future." MacIntyre was beginning to sound like a preacher to Jeff.

"You can't keep me imprisoned in the Realm."

"You've become a narcissist." MacIntyre snorted. "You think you can outwit the entire Realm and its support from The Living World?"

Bandela-Jackson was nose-to-nose with his adversary. Jeff thought he saw sparks flaring between them. Bandela-Jackson snarled in a low, even tone. "You don't know what I've learned." The words hung like threats. "I'll come back here and find a way to live inside the Internet. To regenerate it. To become it. To experience everything. I won't give that up. And I won't have to." Bandela-Jackson emphatically stood his ground. Abruptly they were bombarded by cascading claps of thunder, followed by a sky exploding with lightning bolts. Bandela was demonstrating the power he had amassed by creating a spectacle with it.

Tami-TuMa'Aye Gra'Vay had silently allowed her companions to confront Bandela-Jackson. Now her clear voice rode the brisk wind, carrying a chill and hint of a siren sound. Her outstretched arms gave the appearance of wings about to lift her off the ground. "I summon the power of The Living World. You might recall how it aided me when you attacked me at the pond. That was just a tiny demonstration, Bandela." A jagged bolt of lightning struck next to Bandela-Jackson, who nearly dematerialized in terror. She strode close to him. "That was not one of your tricks that conjure the illusion of lightning. It was The Living World speaking directly to you," she stated. Bandela-Jackson cowered.

    ■   ■   ■

TuMa'Aye Gra'Vay had chosen to retain her Tami Graves persona. But when they wound their way through the park toward the fountain she had felt the evil potency of an overbearing power. Doubt and foreboding crept through her. When Bandela-Jackson had approached she was shocked by his wildly pulsating aura; it was unlike any she had encountered. It shot out fiery red sparks and danced with vivid strands of jet black and brown. It took a moment for her to focus and respond to the persona he presented. He had perfected the debonair sophisticate who aptly uttered sarcasm and ridicule with a sense of superiority. Slowly, however, the familiar Bandela personality broke through. Yet this creature, who in the Realm had seemed innocuous, comical in his bombastic manner and inability to hold a persona, now exuded evil. It was a ghastly contrast.

Tami-TuMa'Aye Gra'Vay studied him as he interacted with her companions, observing an unplanned strategy working effectively as Bandela-Jackson taunted her entourage, even as he was challenged by each of them. She was especially proud of Jeff and Marie. Her group had deftly turned the situation into a face-saving way out for Bandela as MacIntyre outlined the potential plan for Bandela's future. The renegade leader was not ready to capitulate. As his lightning show commenced, Tami-TuMa'Aye Gra'Vay noticed Jeff and Marie retreating slightly. She sensed their terror. At the same time, Henderson and MacIntyre closed ranks with her, poised to counter an attack.

The storm intensified and Tami-TuMa'Aye Gra'Vay was reminded of the attack on her at the pond. That night the natural world around her had come to her aid. A demonstration of the power of The Living World. Now Bandela-Jackson was attempting to use natural forces against her but she knew that what they witnessed was only a projection from Bandela-Jackson himself. He could not seize and use the powers of Nature. It was just a show. She now felt The Living World pulsating around her and confronted Bandela-Jackson with the force of a mighty bolt that sizzled, forming steam on the concrete.

As he cowered and his image wavered, Tami-TuMa'Aye Gra'Vay sought the center of the renegade's power. She was surprised to find not one source but many, and a negative pull from within that was straining Bandela-Jackson's ability. The absorbed Synons were trying to resist. She burrowed deeper, feeling their combined feeble yet persistent strength fusing with hers. It took only a moment for Henderson and MacIntyre to comprehend what was happening and join her. Bandela-Jackson could not maintain his hold. His three opponents began extracting the trapped Synons singly and in groups, drawing them into their own massive power field. Voices whispered as a perception of Synon entities engulfed Tami-TuMa'Aye Gra'Vay. Her human companions, who had moved backward, stood huddled together. She heard their gasps of astonishment.

The pool of light from the moon had expanded, revealing the expanse of Tami- TuMa'Aye Gra'Vay's aura. Scintillating, it shimmered; portions detached and whirled as if in a frantic dance to unheard music. The whirls coalesced into the human personas of those Bandela had absorbed. Tami-TuMa'Aye Gra'Vay recognized George and Miriam Jordan and the Synons who had been lost in the recent battle, including Alana. There were many other Synons who had been released.

"Come, Synons. You're safe now." Tami Graves spoke in TuMa'Aye Gra'Vay's voice.

They reluctantly moved closer to where she now stood with her own group, warily eying Bandela-Jackson. MacIntyre and Henderson approached Alana and the others from the recent battle, shaking hands and embracing them. The Synons who had stood in reserve now moved to form a protective band around their queen and her companions. But they were not met with the expected retaliation.

Jackson's persona was fluctuating, reforming. His aura was irregular, now dominated by grays and dull black. Suddenly, a short, portly bald man with a nose like a pig's snout stood before them. "Oink. It's me, Bandela," he muttered sheepishly.

He tried to project reckless nonchalance. "You got me for now. Didn't see that coming at all. But I will regain potency." The released Synons, some who had been held for a long time, recoiled from him.

"It's alright, people," Bandela conceded. "I won't do it again. I promise, no more absorbing." He barked a laugh. "Synons are unable to lie, huh? So, Queenie. I need your assurance of fair treatment. Looks like I'm temporarily your prisoner." His image flickered slightly as his renegade voice seeped out. "Temporarily." Then the porcine illusion solidified.

Henderson turned his attention to the newly freed flock. "Were you aware?" He looked as if he feared the answer.

"No," one replied. "Once he was able to suppress our initial struggling, it was like we were hibernating, unconscious. We were awoken by an external power."

"That power was wielded by Queen TuMa'Aye Gra'Vay." Henderson bowed toward her. "She will see that Bandela does no more harm."

Bandela sighed in mock resignation. "It was fun while it lasted, being a mysterious renegade leader. I have to say it was getting a little burdensome. Maybe it's not yet time for my plan to work."

"If your plan is harmful, we will never allow it to unfold." MacIntyre interjected sternly.

Bandela's entire demeanor altered. He whined, "I just want to live in the Internet. Not have to worry about fabricating a body. Learn everything. I'm an archivist, after all. This is humankind's ultimate archive."

Was this a ploy or was he recognizing his predicament? Tami-TuMa'Aye Gra'Vay challenged him. "That's a far stretch from wanting to rule the world as a new entity. You have time on your side. Perhaps you can work with humans to build something marvelous for them and you. Achieve something even greater than you are now imagining."

Bandela attempted to bluster. "You're just trying to use the human carrot and stick tactic. You plan to keep me in a force field or something."

MacIntyre reminded him that the "stick" was ever present. "You're right. Until you prove trustworthy, you will be closely guarded. You'll never be allowed to repeat this calamity. If you try it, you'll meet with disaster. Remember, The Living World protects itself and you have been threatening evolutionary order." MacIntyre's human persona loomed over Bandela.

Bandela's countenance bore abject dejection. "My options are bleak. Perhaps you should just absorb me now."

"Bandela." TuMa'Aye Gra'Vay stepped closer to him, motioning MacIntyre away. Everyone else warily kept their distance except Henderson, who moved up behind her. Bandela sat on the pavement, head down. "Bandela." She repeated his name. "Can you bring back Dr. Jackson? I'd really like to talk to him."

"I don't know if I can," he squeaked. He clambered to his feet and adopted a look of concentration. His figure wavered a bit, but nothing happened. He sank back down with a thud. "It's so taxing being Dr. Jackson, and even more arduous being the renegade leader. But I can't tolerate being pig-snout Bandela."

The human and Synon contingent stared at the pitiful spectacle before them. Could this entity have recently threatened the very evolutionary order? Tami-TuMa'Aye Gra'Vay recognized the classic traits that humans often identified as mental illness. Bandela had gone from megalomaniacal narcissism to self-loathing depression. It was disconcerting to realize that her own kind could be susceptible to this condition in such a pronounced way.

Henderson addressed Bandela. "MacIntyre can really lecture, but there's substance in what he says. We can find a way to get you back to the Realm to reconstitute yourself. You need the restorative calm there. Then we can examine what might be the best path. It will be easy to send Dr. Jackson on sabbatical for a while."

Tami-TuMa'Aye Gra'Vay was shocked when Jeff interrupted. "He has to fix our computer software. Immediately," he demanded.

That seemed to be the jolt of inspiration that Bandela needed. He looked up at Jeff and started climbing to his feet. "You'll be amazed." His persona rippled and a strange figure appeared: a thin, pale young man with a swipe of auburn beard across his chin and a shock of unruly red hair, portions sticking straight up and others dropping over one eye. A gold earring dangled from one ear. "Hi. I'm—who am I? Name, someone? For your new hacker wizard? Hey, Josh Jackson. Gabe's son. Okay?" He grinned. The voice was youthful; the tone betrayed no hint of sarcasm or derision.

Smiles broke out among humans and Synons alike. Despite their deep distrust of the entity before them, they were caught up in the enthusiasm the young man oozed.

Tami-TuMa'Aye Gra'Vay glanced at MacIntyre, whose eyes glittered, but not with relief or joy. The wheels were visibly turning; clearly he was devising tactics for containing the inner core lurking beneath the surface of this promising persona. His vow that Bandela's renegade plans would never unfold was unwavering.

Henderson stepped forward and shook the young man's hand. "Welcome to the world, Josh. We'll get to work right away, first we have something else to take care of."

* * *

The fountain they were before was on the top of a rise that gently sloped to open grassy fields designed for large gatherings. Out of the surrounding trees a faint glow appeared. A mass of figures emerged onto the grass. They looked like people but their auras were brightly illuminated, forming a luminous halo over the entire group. As they approached, Tami-TuMa'Aye Gra'Vay began walking toward them, followed by Henderson and MacIntyre.

"Wha…" Marie looked at Jeff, who stood transfixed watching the throng.

He smiled down at her and put his arm around her shoulders. "I think we are two humans among many…"

"Synons." She finished his sentence. "I can almost sense them. Of course, the auras help."

"I guess this is the back-up army that was recruited from surrounding areas. Wow. I wonder how many there are all over the world. This is amazing."

"Mind-blowing," she said. "We are honored, I think. We'll never be able to talk about this, will we?"

"I guess we have to stick close together then." Jeff leaned down and kissed her soft blond hair. "What's that?" He felt something warm and soft against his legs. Looking down, he found a sleek black cat gazing up at him with vivid green eyes. "Hello? Who are you?"

Jeff jerked as a thought swept through his mind. "I'm Cat. Tami said you'd take care of me. Well, she didn't exactly say you, but I can sense you're the person she told me about."

Jeff stood immobilized, stunned. Then logical thought returned. Tami can do a lot, especially implanting thoughts in minds. I think this is the message I needed. He gently picked up the cat, who yielded without a struggle. "Marie, meet Cat. We're going to give him a home."

She reached over and stroked the silky head as Cat turned his wise green eyes on Marie. She felt no urge to question what had just happened. "We?" she said coyly. Their eyes met with a profound knowledge that their life had changed forever. A smile tugged at the corner of her mouth. "I can do that." A stirring in the atmosphere turned their attention back to their surroundings. Cat snuggled into Jeff's arms, purring loudly.

Tami-TuMa'Aye Gra'Vay was still on the rise above the throng. She raised her arms to them and spoke, her clear voice resounding across the meadow. "Welcome, Synons. Thank you for answering our call for aid. I'm pleased to tell you that the conflict has been resolved peacefully. This is a rare and special occasion, however. I doubt that this number of us has ever before been assembled on this plane. I was completely unaware that so many of us were living as humans here, and that is my flaw. Clearly, for you, it is a means to further our mission and I want to learn from each of you. While we are here together tonight we will bond and share knowledge. It will be the first of many such conclaves, large and small, to ensure that we maintain our connection and use our shared experienced to aid each other, this world, and The Living World."

Tami-TuMa'Aye Gra'Vay began to glow and shimmer, then dissolve. A vivid rainbow aura momentarily blinded Jeff and Marie before the Deer Woman appeared in their midst, hair flying. TuMa'Aye Gra'Vay wore two faces, one bore the look of a human Everywoman, beautiful in a universal way. The other face was a doe, which rapidly changed to a myriad of animal faces, then to that of a young girl. TuMa'Aye Gra'Vay flung open her brilliant rainbow cloak to encompass everyone, beckoning to Bandela's terrified renegade accomplices, who sat quietly in the shadows beside the fountain, to join them. "We are Synons. We are spirit guides, maintaining and strengthening humanity's bond with The Living World. All living things are our family. We are one."

EPILOGUE

Josh Jackson sat at the small desk, fingers flying over the keys of an antiquated manual typewriter. He sat in a small cage with mesh-like metal walls, floors, and ceiling. The cage was within a larger windowless room patrolled by soldiers in full combat gear. They included humans and Synons who had chosen to assume the same appearance. As Josh completed several pages he slid them through a slit in his cage; then they were collected and rushed through the heavy fortified doors to a team of high-echelon scientists and technicians. They painstakingly analyzed the material and passed on instructions for repairing the municipal network Bandela had revamped to Jeff Hawke and his cyber team.

After Bandela's new Josh Jackson persona was secured, Jeff was invited to visit the facility and participate in establishing procedures.

Jeff had never seen a Faraday cage, the enclosure that now shielded Bandela-Josh from electricity, depriving him of a means to use or increase his power. Nor had Jeff ever been inside a lead lined state-of-the-art bomb shelter, the greater enclosure in which the renegade Synon who had transformed into Josh Jackson was imprisoned.

Bandela had planted extraordinary possibilities within the city's network, so advanced—but with dangerous potential—that only a select few human and Synon personas with top clearance knew of its existence. Most of the pages that flew from Josh Jackson's typewriter, and the corresponding cyber code as it was removed from the municipal network, would be sequestered within a maximum-security vault to lie dormant shielded by the most formidable protection. The material would be continuously assessed, and as human technology progressed, relevant chunks of Bandela's data would be released and implemented.

■　　■　　■

TuMa'Aye Gra'Vay was astonished at the number of Synons residing on Earth. She was true to her word, meeting with those who had answered the call for help, learning from them and helping them establish networks to stay in touch instead of being isolated in small, secretive groups.

Yet, as she worked to learn about and assist Earth-dwelling Synons, she grappled with the many ways this experience had changed her. Her Tami Graves persona had leapt into twenty-first century human civilization and absorbed a tremendous amount of its knowledge. Her persona had become so like humans in body and mind that it felt like an evolutionary step. That prospect was exhilarating, but perplexing and alarming. In this short time, she had developed emotions and sensations Synons had always assumed were the sole province of biological creatures. What did that portend for the multitude of Synons living as humans? It could have profound effects.

In her conferences with Earth-Synons, she subtly attempted to ascertain the extent of their emotional growth, but it seemed that they had avoided close relationships with people, forming "families" of their own kind. She warned them to continue to resist emotional ties with humans. Perhaps her own experience had been a very isolated situation, perpetuated by the goal she had set herself and the methods she employed to gain Jeff Hawke's trust. Obviously, her ignorance had led to unintended consequences.

TuMa'Aye Gra'Vay only hoped that Jeff's potential for trust had not been irreparably damaged. She was heartened that he had Marie and Cat to love and support him as he trod a new path that would lead to even more astounding revelations. He represented an untouched human potential. She had no doubt that many others with his unique capabilities existed on Earth. They must be located and developed. Humans who revered their bond with The Living World were vital to Earth's survival.

TuMa'Aye Gra'Vay was wise and resilient. She could use this experience to grow and aid other Synons in their missions involving people. Longing for the serenity of the Realm, she returned as soon as it was apparent that the Earth-Synons had moved into a new and positive phase and that the renegade Bandela was under control.

For the multitude of Earth-dwelling Synons a new era of acknowledgment by and cooperation with the Realm generated renewed dedication to nurturing the Earth and its inhabitants' connection to The Living World.

But were they too late?

* * *

PROLOGUE TO BOOK TWO OF THE LIVING WORLD SERIES

The Realm shuddered and vibrated. It was a place that was not a true place, a universe held together by the collective beings that inhabited it, called Synons. They struggled to stay intact, reaching inward for strength and outward for connection. They had never known terror, although they had witnessed it countless times in the inhabitants of Earth. Now a visceral understanding of that biological reaction spread through them. Their purpose was to maintain and strengthen the link between The Living World that encompassed all of Creation and the living things on Earth, especially the dominant species, humans. That link needed constant reinforcement; it was fraying at an accelerated rate that threatened the very existence of the Realm.

The Realm was bathed in a pulsating kaleidoscope of colors, dominated by pastels, punctuated by shafts and orbs of deep primary hues. In an instant, the energy-mind-spirit that comprised the Synons unified in one undulating motion, a tranquil rhythm that linked the many as one, but their fragile union was assailed by waves of turbulence.

A collective wail reverberated through the Synons' connection to Earth. The Living Earth was in anguish and lashing out.

■　■　■

*To continue reading, look for Book Two, **Precarious.***
Coming soon.

ACKNOWLEDGMENTS

I'm grateful to all those who have helped me in the development of this book: family; my colleagues/friends in Write On! Writers; and others who have encouraged and advised me, especially in the North Carolina Writers Network.

Special thanks to Susan Snowden for editorial assistance and to Michelle Owen for book and cover design.

Our cover image is a detail from a stunning assemblage of 48 frames taken with Hubble Space Telescope's Advanced Camera for Surveys of the Carina Nebula, NGC3372, which is within our own Milky Way Galaxy, 7,500 light years away. It show stars in the process of formation.

Please visit **https://esahubble.org/** for more information and to view breathtaking images from the Hubble Space Telescope. As one of humankind's major innovations, this space-based observatory provides unprecedented knowledge and research opportunities. A collaboration between ESA (European Space Agency) and NASA, it's an example of what international cooperation can accomplish.

AUTHOR AFTERWORD

I am fortunate to live within a day trip of Cherokee, North Carolina, home of the Eastern Band of the Cherokee Indians. I have enjoyed and learned much from the museums, village, outdoor drama, and books purchased there. Visit: (**https://visitcherokeenc.com/**) All references to Native American culture are made in the highest regard and I apologize for any errors or misleading inferences.

This book is set in NC's Research Triangle (**https://www. researchtriangle.org/the-triangle/**) From the site: "The Research Triangle gets its name from Research Triangle Park and three Tier 1 research universities—Duke University, North Carolina State University, and the University of North Carolina Chapel Hill—located only minutes apart." The three cities of Durham, Chapel Hill, and Raleigh (state capital) are sometimes informally called by this title as do my characters in dialogue. I've taken "poetic liberty" to invent fictional locations and dramatic incidents for the sake of my narrative, and I apologize for any misconceptions.

Some of my characters are avid science fiction fans and talk about real science fiction characters, television shows, movies, comics, etc. These references are made in the spirit of "homage" or tribute.

The scientific references are based on real and theoretically postulated principles and practices. If they tweak your interest, please research to learn more about them.

The character and name of TuMa'Aye Gra'Vay sprang up in my childhood imagination as a faery queen and somehow nestled in my mind for decades until she made me again acknowledge her. Her first published literary incarnation was under the name "Tumai" in "Faery Fading" (Fantasy winner), Third Annual Fiction Anthology of Genre Contest Winners **https://www.amazon.com/dp/B00E9JC33K/ ref=dp-kindle-redirect?_encoding=UTF8&btkr=1**

She demanded a new identity that, impelled by my concern for the threat humans pose to all of Earth's life, led to my science fiction series The Living World. You'll revisit most of the Passageway characters and meet new ones in the next books.

Thanks to all who read this series. It's meant as entertaining speculative fiction, but I hope it prompts readers to a renewed appreciation of Nature and resolve to do whatever seems appropriate and feasible to help our unique Earth and the life she nourishes.

I hope you enjoyed this first installment of The Living World series. A review on Amazon or other sites would help me to build on what worked in this book and make the future installments even more satisfying to my readers. Please visit our seaofmountainspress.com website or my Patricia Vestal, Author Facebook page for links and information on this and upcoming books.

ABOUT THE AUTHOR

Patricia Vestal's career encompasses publishing and higher education. She earned her Communications BA from State University of New York and an MA in Drama from New York University. She's a member of the North Carolina Writers Network, the Dramatists Guild and the Alliance of Independent Authors. In addition to readings, stage and television productions of her plays, Patricia's publications include fiction, reviews, and essays. She now conducts writing workshops and courses in her home state of North Carolina, whose mountains, rich Native American roots, and high-tech Research Triangle inspired the setting and characters for Passageways, the first book in her series The Living World.

ABOUT PASSAGEWAYS

Shape-shifting energy beings, a universe tethered to Earth, enigmatic cyberattackers, telepathic animals, and diverse people populate **Passageways**, Book One of **The Living World** science-fiction series.

A trio of personalities is drawn into a mind-bending adventure: Jeff Hawke left his Cherokee people in North Carolina's mountains to work as a cyber security tech in the state's urban Research Triangle, where he's confronted with the challenge of his life; Tami Graves is investigating cutting edge artificial intelligence for a science magazine; Synon Queen TuMa'Aye Gra'Vay arrives on Earth from the Realm seeking the source of threats to the Synon mission of maintaining humanity's diminishing link to The Living World. Their paths touch, catapulting them into a vortex of hurdles and peril that compel them to confront inner selves and outer forces that threaten catastrophic consequences.

A self-contained story, **Passageways** sets the stage for the astounding revelations and events of the subsequent entries in **The Living World** series. Watch for Book Two soon.